Alexander Hay Japp

Three Great Teachers of Our Own Time

Being an Attempt to Deduce the Spirit and Purpose Animating Carlyle, Tennyson

and Ruskin

Alexander Hay Japp

Three Great Teachers of Our Own Time
Being an Attempt to Deduce the Spirit and Purpose Animating Carlyle, Tennyson and Ruskin

ISBN/EAN: 9783337058746

Printed in Europe, USA, Canada, Australia, Japan

Cover: Foto ©Raphael Reischuk / pixelio.de

More available books at **www.hansebooks.com**

THREE GREAT TEACHERS

OF OUR OWN TIME:

BEING

AN ATTEMPT TO DEDUCE THE SPIRIT AND PURPOSE

ANIMATING

CARLYLE, TENNYSON AND RUSKIN.

BY

ALEXANDER H. JAPP.

LONDON:

SMITH, ELDER AND CO., 65, CORNHILL.

1865.

PREFACE.

THESE essays were composed mostly in the intervals of arduous professional duty. The writer states this not with any idea of forestalling criticism; but rather that his readers may know that the task has been taken up *con amore*. The nature of the views advanced, and the persistent attempts made to find out and to fix not only the progressive unity of life and work in each of our three great writers—Carlyle, Tennyson and Ruskin;—but a unity also of spirit and purpose binding them together into a suggestive trio, will, he fondly hopes, favourably recommend them to the daily-augmenting ranks of the thoughtful and inquiring. At any rate the author commits his volume trustfully to the hands of those who may be interested in any worthy word spoken regarding either or all of them.

But indeed when one thinks of the great need there

is for a wide-based reform in our extravagant ways of thought, and above all, in our foolish and empty habits of life, he cannot but wish that the influence of these three—an influence so directed towards drawing men back to truthfulness, simplicity and genuine affection in all the relations of life—could be brought very widely to bear. For though men "run to and fro" and by that means truly knowledge is being increased, yet with the knowledge the curse comes ever, sending men thirsty and fevered to wander over the wide arid desert of "circumstance," there only to fail grievously in the search for blessedness in all forms of external finery and falseness. This is the price we pay for progress; the tax the grim tollman of civilization exacts of us. But in everything there is compensation. Sour smoke has possibility in it to become clear lambent flame. The artificial involvements of our time may be transmuted into pathways of return to primitive repose, simplicity, and fruitfulness. They who can and will, at great self-sacrifice, direct us wisely in this matter, surely deserve not only grateful recognition but "blessings and eternal praise." Carlyle, Tennyson, and Ruskin have taken upon themselves to prescribe the cure for the "vague disease" of the century.

Surely then it more and more behoves us to try to discover what these, our three great men, really mean—to get at the root-principle, the spirit out of which they write; and if it be a true one, then to practically adjust, not only our words and thoughts, but also our acts and lives thereby. This is the claim they have over us as thinking men if they are indeed our Great Teachers. The writer finds they are one in aim and spirit and desire. Their words may vary slightly, but they soon resolve themselves into one grand all-including monition :— "Be simple, single-minded, prudent, true, genuine men." They are pre-eminently a sort of missionaries these three, preaching each in his own way, according to opportunity, truths old as the Old Testament; but practically forgotten and departed from. Broadly taken, one may say they separate themselves from nearly all the other writers of the time by the fact that they have each asserted their place in literature without the sacrifice of their individuality. As they value their specific character and distinctive qualities as men, so do they reverence these in others—making the maintenance of them the very basis of the great reform they unitedly aim at accomplishing. Through individual regeneration and intense personal conviction, all improvement that is worthy is to be accomplished; consequently there is nothing narrow, dogmatic or sectarian about their writings; but a noble universality of thought and spirit throughout. Individual goodness is with them the root of all progress and of all national prosperity. It is the little seed-grain which grows into a great world-tree, spreading grateful shadow for thousands.

Our very external culture is cursing us they say, by sucking away all true individuality of life or of conviction; producing thus an over-refinement whose children are desire, unrest, sensualism, and barbaric trust in material resources. The respect for individuality felt by these men soon accordingly transforms them into art-critics essentially, as seen from one point of view. They discover an element of cold pagan intellectualism, opposed alike to true progress and true Christianity, sapping away the lives of men or making them fruitless, empty and diseased. They enter on a contest for maintaining the sacredness of life. That contest under varying names, and assuming in different circumstances different features, is traceable throughout all Christian history. It may be said to simply circle round the question whether or not art in its lower or heathen form shall be called in to decorate and sen-

suously limit Christian doctrine ; or in other words, the
meaning of the higher facts of human existence. This
may seem a very paradoxical way of putting the matter ;
but it is not the less the true one. For all religious struggles ultimately resolve themselves into these questions
—What is true art ? and what are its relations to true
religion ? All down the stream of time we see men
struggling for some clear solution of this problem, and
actually leaving real work undone in the hope of obtain-
ing a satisfactory settlement of it. It is the perennial
difficulty this—the reconciliation of man's higher aspirations with the circumstances out of which he has to
shape a form for the fitting expression of these—a form.
which shall not be remote, unreal, or distant on the one
hand, nor hard, materialised, and pagan on the other.
Indeed, properly speaking, the idea of a State or civil
order implies a Church, and that again implies art. If
men meet they must have symbols—the very forms of
your church doors or windows will crystallize themselves
into expressions of spiritual experiences, and therefore
you must guard against the introduction of any material element which will have in itself the tendency to
drag the spirit earthward simply by being constantly
before it.

A great moral and spiritual reform, from whatever point it takes its departure, will thus very soon of necessity carry itself into the region of art. It was not out of a desire of destruction merely that Cromwell and his soldiers so ruthlessly destroyed the art in the churches they entered in Scotland and in Ireland. That other reformer enunciated a deep principle when he said, "Pull down the nests lest the crows come back to them!" An art that forms round about a system will have some vital affinity to it, and will be apt even by being looked upon to stimulate feelings akin to those out of which the system sprang and which intensely characterized the devotees. The immobile dreamy nature of the Hindoo first of all expressed in his religion and his philosophy would yet have some freedom, some possibility of *otherness*, if the expression may be pardoned; but when one man of gift above his fellows formed one of these ugly abnormal figures, the worst and weakest characteristics of the people would be objectified, confirmed, and fixed. And so it comes that a high and noble reform must soon interfere with art. Even Plato would exclude certain poets from his Republic. The heroic Savonarola could not long escape, after he had entered on his career of reform, the necessity of becoming iconoclast. And so he thundered out his protests against the debauched Medicis and sensualized sons of the Vatican, telling them that the pictures on the walls of their churches and convents were for the pleasure of the eye only and lured the soul to death by satiating the senses. The Virgin he boldly declared was never arrayed as they dressed and ornamented her,—"I tell you," he proceeds, "she walked about clothed as a humble, simple, young woman." And when he railed at poets and artists for the manner in which they followed heathen writers and slavishly copied heathen forms he only expressed a fact over which multitudes of good men have mourned in all times. When John Knox pitched the figure of the Virgin into the water, to see if it would swim, he proved the futility of the introduction of half-pagan art for the illustration of such sublime subjects by an immediate appeal to the stern facts of nature. Both these directly declared against the divorce of art from fact, reality and life; and refused to sanction the application of the products of debased and sensual minds in any way to the inter-pretation of Divine ideas.

As reformers of a broad vital order our Great Teachers are also, as has been said, in one point of view and by necessity essentially art-critics, loudly calling men back to fact, simplicity, and truth—those eternal laws of nature sympathy with which alone can give lastingness to any piece of work from the building of the lowliest wall to the painting of the sublimest picture of a Raphael or an Angelico. A Carlyle, when he comes to face most directly the practical questions of the day, sweeps grimly through the atmosphere of art, and with reprobations almost amounting to curses rising at times into a whirl-wind of fiery sarcasm, he proclaims from too prominent indications discernible that Jesuitism is no longer a thing of doctrine or of sect, but has become an accepted law of life and art and work. A Tennyson, too, lives in constant revolt against our artistic-sensualism or worship of the dæmonic-beautiful; and from the moment he indited his *Palace of Art* till now his voice has been quietly, gently raised in protest; emphatic and earnest withal if protest ever was. And John Ruskin's life-purpose, to which he has solemnly consecrated himself as of old did the heroes who went forth to search for the San Graal, is to proclaim, like another John, the law of simplicity and truth—the law of honesty and holiness and beauty of life as the basis and only fountain-head of all that can ever become great and enduring in art.

Our teachers do not deal with arbitrary forms to re-generate *them*. They protest against that sort of reform also; and hence to the old they sometimes appear so very contradictory and opposed to order. The men who have fought as *priests* have mostly failed, or at best but partially succeeded in their end. Is it not an indisputable fact that even Luther became the parent of a Lutheranism in some points nearly as much needing to be dissented from as Romanism itself? And did not Savonarola grow perplexed amid his dialectical formulas and his martyrologies, and good great man as he was, spoiled thus his mighty work and retarded the reformation he so burned to bring about; and all because he *would* remain essentially a priest? Edward Irving, the Savonarola of our century, tried also to purify the world by first regenerating church formulas, and every one knows how that noble soul went down in mist and darkness amid the wreck of his powers and crushed by the thought of crippled aspirations. Coleridge, too, tried the same thing, though from the more philosophical standpoint; and his failure is perhaps more portentous and mournful than that of any other man either before or since.

This, in short, is the glory of our teachers, that they

are not *priests* but men—good brave men—of the laity yet *reverent;* appointed for their task, divinely in a sense too, and that task they hold by with a purpose and a decision alike honouring to them and to us; each working in his particular way as if solemnly consecrated for his work and for nothing else.

A. H. J.

London, June 10*th,* 1865.

CONTENTS.

———◆◇◆———

THREE GREAT TEACHERS.

THOMAS CARLYLE,

HIS MISSION AND INFLUENCE.

CLASSIFICATION in these days has literally run mad. As we bottle up our different chemical elements, and label them separately and severally, for the better practical service afterwards, so would we do with human souls, if we could. When a new book appears, the author must be classified, preparatory even to his being reviewed; when a new truth is attained, it is only accepted in so far as it can be made a new label under which other things are to be hereafter for a time ranged and distributed. In short, we are much too scientific and unpoetical, in the true sense of that word, and shortsightedly carry our notions derived from the material sphere into the spiritual also. Thereby we

1

do great mischief, and retard real progress. For even our classifications of nature are not, and must not be regarded as final; but only as more or less approximately true, needing to be constantly revised : and, consequently, new arrangements and distributions of our accumulated resources are inevitable and certain. Nature, too, is spiritual and inexhaustible, and resolutely refuses to be treated of as mechanical merely; and hence the perpetual noisy pother about new discoveries, rival sections in science, and so forth. If, then, the rigidly conservative classifying tendency has done mischief in the physical, how much more must it have done so when carried into the moral and spiritual! Our metaphysics and theology alike 'tend to make us more sturdy labellers than even our material science, driving us to dwell and rejoice in sectional and half-false views of things, so that we threaten to become even blind to the broad, the inclusive, the universal, the human. The first question the theologians put of a book, or of a man either, is not whether the book is good and the spirit high; or of the man—is he a nobly struggling, devout, pious soul; but rather is he or it Calvinistic or Arminian ? The metaphysicians in the same way question—Is he or it Baconian or Berkeleyan, Hegelian or Hamiltonian ? Finding that the book or the man does not happen to be either, then from all the various points of the shifting compass of criticism come blasts of condemnation.

Perhaps no single English writer has caused more
perplexity to the classifying mind than Thomas Carlyle.
He resolutely refused to range himself under any label
whatever, and it was not till a few spirits began to name
themselves Carlyleans that the labellers even deigned to
return to the subject. They thought they had done
with the phenomenon ; had settled it finally by rejecting
it, and declaring it nothing ! And now they are about
as surprised that Carlyle, as he declined to range himself under some old category, now likewise declines to
become himself a label, though he is flattered by being told
that he well deserves such a place on the shelf. He
persists rather in extending himself out on all sides
of his nature, in such a way indeed that he would be
certain to crack the scientific bottle were he ever forced
inside it !

Such distinctions as that between analytical and
synthetical minds—between logical and imaginative—
between one class that constructs to recommend the
truth and another that breaks up with the self-same
end—need not therefore be ventured on here with the
purpose of assigning Thomas Carlyle definitively to either.
The fact is all men of the highest type belong to both
classes—combine in themselves the best of both characters. The logical faculty and the imaginative faculty so
called are in truth but sides of the individual nature,
or channels through which it expresses itself. Either
of them may be depressed or unduly developed ; and

when that is the case a man, for the sake of distinction
merely, is spoken of as belonging to the one class or the
other. All our grander men, as has been said, combine
both characters. A keener eye, a more thoroughly
inquiring, compacter intellect than Luther's we have not
witnessed ; and yet his daily life of struggle and endeavour was influenced to a quite inappreciable degree by
the visions which he saw or believed he saw. Shakspeare,
we can discover, was a keen critic. From the little we
know of his intercourse with others, we may conclude
that he possessed the essential elements for one—
quiet, patient, kindly study of character ; the utmost
toleration, unassumingness, and willingness to take the
best out of those he met with. And, as I am bold to maintain, that all true criticism ultimately resolves itself into
a study of human character—of the moods, conditions,
and obstacles which influenced the creation or the doing
of any great work—it may be safely said that Shakspeare
in those historical plays of his proves himself one of the
most wonderful of critics. Then Goethe's name is sure
to suggest itself after that of Shakspeare. Was not
Goethe a man of science, subtle in analysis, full of
knowledge as precise and direct, too, as that of any man
of his day—a perfect miscellany of facts and separate
truths ; in short, a discoverer, an inventor, and how
much more ? And yet, so far as is known, he never
regretted the development of that side of genius, but
rather joyed in it, as affording a true foundation on

which to build his realistic fictions. " Plato the wise, and large-browed Verulam," might also be pointed to for proofs and illustrations of this statement; for he would certainly be an acute man who would tell us where the analytical and the imaginative proper began and ended in these two princely souls.

Thomas Carlyle likewise belongs to this lofty brotherhood of "clear and universal men." He possesses one of the subtlest and most penetrating intellects; in any department of abstract inquiry he would have succeeded; indeed, his high distinction in both branches of mathematics while yet a young man is proof of this. But he would not consent to be one-sided; to himself—to his whole nature he *would* be true, and, therefore, abandoning the prospect of distinction in this special intellectual walk, he at once passed into a field of literary labour which called more into play the whole faculties of mind and soul. The mathematical and metaphysical have been subordinately serviceable, it is true, helping him frequently to such a striking expression of lofty thought as he could not otherwise have attained; as, for instance, when he carries his algebra into the sublimest region of Christian truth, and tells us in *Sartor* that " *the fraction of life can be increased in value not so much by increasing your numerator as by lessening your denominator.* Nay, unless my algebra deceive me, *Unity* itself divided by *Zero* will give *Infinity.* Make thy claim of wages a Zero, then; thou hast the world under thy feet."

But in proof of this statement, if proof were needed, that Carlyle combines in himself at once the characters of reasoner and poet—critic and creator—one might point to the essays on Voltaire, Burns, Scott, Goethe, Richter, and Diderot. How much patient analysis and careful critical adjustment must have preceded the construction or rather creation (for in each case the picture seems to have fused itself into poetic coherency in the mind of the writer even before he put pen to paper) of these surprisingly real and life-like portraits, of men, too, of so different and, indeed, almost irreconcilable types of character; and yet where nought is extenuated and nought set down in malice. The fact of such a mass of complete biographies in little of so many men separated from each other by such definite and distinctive marks, of itself indicates the presence of a surprising faculty— the more that a unity of moral purpose runs through them, like a golden thread, significantly binding them together into one great biographical work, wherein each individual type is simply as a little window through which great and vital principles are powerfully reflected. In all of the essays alike it is found, on a closer study, that the higher faculties of the mind, in the ordinary sense of that expression, are made willing servants to other qualities of a moral sort, which had been to a great extent lost sight of in literature in the desire, which had almost become a disease, to attain on all occasions external grace, fluency, and frippery fineness

of style. Impartiality, honesty, and determined truthfulness are the evident characteristics of these essays.
The writer, beyond all possibility of question, had set
himself right with the subject, had seen clearly into it,
and got, in a sense to love it, before he would engage
to treat of it at all. Thus, although the reader may
sometimes disagree with the opinions of the essayist, he
cannot fail to admire the evident heartiness, enthusiasm,
and earnestness with which he has set about his task.
But even in those essays grace and beauty of style are
by no means lacking. These, however, are felt to arise
directly from the spirit in which the matter is handled ;
and a careful reader soon discovers that the style is just
the most fitting possible for the purpose—so that
manner as well as spirit at length comes to impress us
with thorough insight, sincerity, and singleness of aim.

If the co-existence of two broadly separate intellectual faculties is to be recognized at all, a surprising
union of them will be found in the *French Revolution*,
which work is essentially the gathering into one great
centre of the two lines of thought Mr. Carlyle may be
said to have described in his keen reflections upon man
—his fine arts and social arrangements. What it chiefly
concerns us to remark here, however, is that in this
wonderful " epic of History," or panoramic illustration
of great historical principles, the writer shows everywhere evidence of the most assiduous study and the
most carefully minute analysis. He cannot rest satis-

fied with any fact till he has traced its origin in some remote motive or passion. Society in the abstract he will have nought to do with. If you speak of " the masses," he retorts, " Masses, indeed : and yet singular to say, if, with an effort of imagination, thou follow them, over broad France, into their clay hovels, into their garrets and hutches, the masses consist all of units. Every unit of whom has his own heart and sorrows ; stands there covered with his own skin, and if you prick him he will bleed." And so constantly, by the most unusual and amazing turns, he resolves all that is general and threatens to become abstract into living essences and persons, and will not be content with any historical result till he has dived into the depths and brought from thence a human soul, all undreamt of before, who must, willingly or unwillingly, stand sponsor to it. That is his peculiarity and confirmed manner of working. He is like the sculptor who needs to study the anatomy of the human frame in health and in disease before he can truthfully shape out the proportions either of a majestic Apollo or a rude Faun, develope the gracefully flowing curvatures of a Venus, or the contorted grimacings of a Triton. The artist differs from the anatomist only in so far as he analyses with set purpose of constructing. But, indeed, properly speaking, the other does essentially the same thing ; for would that man not be accounted a debased wretch and " enemy of the human race " whose anatomical researches had no reference to human healing, by helping the better diagnosis of disease? So here, practically, we find the two functions of analyst and constructor go together; and are only profitable when they act in soft and subdued harmony. And as with the anatomist, so with Carlyle; he can restore and re-construct so wonderfully because he has followed out his analytical study with such pertinacity and vigour, and anew presents us with the spirit of half-forgotten periods because he has traced facts and results to their roots in human passion, sentiment, and aspiration.

Carlyle's recipiency, his breadth of nature, or, in other words, his complete toleration, is remarkable from the first. Unlike some writers, who run after and can only fairly limn out one type of manhood to which they themselves bear a sort of friendly affinity, Carlyle seems alike at home with a Robespierre or a Luther; with a feeble wavering Louis Caput, or an irrepressible, lion-like Danton; with a softly inquiring mystically-musical Novalis, or a hateful, squalid Marat; with an intense restrictedly-egotistical Schiller, or a great, irregular mass of manhood like Jean Paul Richter. To all these he tries to do justice; and in great measure succeeds, finding some shadow of good in the worst of them. If practical tolerance of men and their ways— the determination not to be unjust in judging, and the firm resolve to mete out to others such a full measure of consideration as he himself hopes and desires to receive, are lessons constantly needing to be anew brought home to us by living examples, then Carlyle, apart from other benefits conferred, deserves our warmest gratitude for practically showing once more the beauty and the benefit of generosity in judging the characters of other men : and this, in a time of selfish sectarianism, exclusiveness, and bigotry, is no small matter.

But perhaps Carlyle's greatest specialty, after all, is his keen insight. He is eagle-eyed ; nothing whatever escapes him. He fishes up matter of essential meaning and moment from remote and neglected corners, where no one before ever dreamt of its existence. A scrap of discoloured paper which Dryasdust has hastily thrown aside, gives him the key to a whole series of weighty transactions, and the intimate relations of those who figured in them. Across the black, gaping void he flashes a concentrated light like the lantern of a watch-man in remote and unfrequented streets at midnight. And he will be true at once to himself and to those of whom he writes. He will abate not a jot of the facts, whatever allowances he may make for the persons who moved among them. Yet all is done lovingly, tenderly; he does not quote the maxim : "The heart sees farther than the head," without having mastered it practically, and faithfully applied it to his own life and work.

Combined with this keen insight, and, indeed, inseparable from it, is the utmost care, amounting even to scrupulousness, in matters of the merest detail. Nothing is unimportant. This is a doctrine Carlyle constantly enunciates; but what is better than enunciation, however able, he has practically exhibited it in all that he has done. Even in the finishing of his books we see it; such perfect indices and analyses of contents are not to be got from any other author. It is the same when we view him as a thinker. He never loosely or carelessly generalizes, although he possesses vast and rapid powers of generalization. The basis of his nature is rugged, stubborn sense. All the rich glowing flowers of his imagination and fancy—fresh, fantastic, varied as the bloom of some Eastern garden—yet rests firmly based on a solid structure, like rich verdure on the hard persistent granite of his native land. At the end of his first volume of essays he gives some "Fractions," among which are four fables. One of these, in the quaintest, most playful manner, signifies that man should not defy or fight with Providence; and in the summary of contents he gives this so *sensibly-naïve* interpretation, which I think thoroughly Scotch, in more respects than one: —"Before we try to force Providence to 'an alternative,' it were wise to consider *what* the alternative might be." This is physiognomic. With the most amazing whirls he passes from the veriest transcendentalism to the sheerest commonplace, from mazy mysticism to shrewdest sense; in his keen glance broad principles and the simplest facts come close together for a moment and shake hands. Thus it is perhaps that the Germans declare him *ganz Englisch ;* that is, rather realistic and sensible for their taste—too inclined to tie a clog to the feet of speculation and philosophy, as dairymen do to the flighty of their herd, that the lactile wealth may not be wholly lost to them and to the world.

This, in point of fact, is Carlyle's most marked peculiarity—his subtlety of thought, and yet its thorough solidity. With the airiest sweeps he can canvass the whole field of speculation; but, like the doves that we see circling round their cot, he is ever drawing nearer to his home in fact, in reality. The distant and the near in human thought and experience are brought together for a moment; and, mutually wondering, recognize themselves mirrored in each other's eyes. If the poet's business is to reconcile what seems discordant, and to show the essential affinities of apparently opposing elements, then Carlyle is undoubtedly the poet of History. He glances across the ages, and as if by magic brings strangers together as did that lucky pupil of Sais. Events defile before him, and he searches out and arranges them according to secret correspondences; even the unlike willingly interpreting each other for him. He reminds us sometimes of the witches in *Macbeth.* He shows us a few of the queerest, weirdest little specimens ever culled from human annals, and he tells us their strangely inconsistent characteristics as he casts them one by one into his cauldron; and lo, the combined result of the mixture is a prophecy—big with fate for us and for the world.

Truly in his hands all history becomes living. He flashes an irradiating light far across the centuries, and old time-worn truths and ideas once more body themselves forth in strangest guises, and the fruits of them, still seen pouring forth from the womb of Time, are fixed and unmistakeably identified. Old Jewry in its decline thus joins hands with American democracy to demonstrate the worth, real or fancied, of the much-boasted panacea of universal suffrage :—

"Did you never hear, with the mind's ear as well, that fateful Hebrew prophecy, I think the fatefullest of all, which sounds daily through the streets, ' Ou clo ! Ou clo ! '—A certain people, once upon a time, clamorously voted by overwhelming majority, ' Not *he ;* Barabbas, not he ! *Him,* and what he is, and what he deserves we know well enough : a reviler of the chief priests and sacred chancery wigs ; a seditious heretic, physical-force chartist, and enemy of his country and mankind. To the gallows and the cross with him ! Barabbas is our man ; Barabbas, we are for Barabbas ! ' They got Barabbas :—have you well considered what a fund of purblind obduracy, of opaque *flunkeyism* grown truculent and transcendent ; what an eye for the phylacteries and want of eye for the eternal noblenesses, sordid loyalty to prosperous Semblances, and high-treason against the Supreme Fact, such a vote betokens in those

natures? For it was the consummation of a long series
of such; they and their fathers had long kept voting so.
A singular people, who could both produce such divine
men, and then could so stone and crucify them; a people
terrible from the beginning!—Well, they got Barabbas;
and they got of course such guidance as Barabbas and
the like of him could give them; and, of course, they
stumbled ever downwards, and devilwards in their own
stiffnecked way; and—and at this hour after eighteen
centuries of saddest fortune they prophetically sing ' Ou
clo!' in all the cities of the world. Might the world, at
this late hour, but take note of them and understand their
song a little!"

And what still humour he sometimes throws into
the gravest subject. By persistent truthfulness he not
seldom achieves results that the most assiduous art
could never reach. No reader of *Friedrich* can forget
the "Tabagie Parliament," and his reflections upon it.
In the *French Revolution*, too, we have some instances of
the same sort. Here, where death seems to loom darkly
over all the characters he paints with such fidelity and
clearness as they march past, and where the horror is
alone relieved by the firm faith the writer holds in good
issues for all times being educed out of the seething
cauldron of revolution, he gives some play to his cunning
humour. Notice in the following lines how gently
he deals with the poor pirate Paul Jones :—

" On thee too, for country's sake, O Chevalier John

Paul, be a word spent, or misspent! In faded naval uni-
form, Paul Jones lingers visible here; like a wine-skin
from which the wine is all drawn. Like the ghost of himself! Low is his once loud bruit; scarcely audible, save,
with extreme tedium, in ministerial ante-chambers, in
this or the other charitable dining-room, mindful of the
past. What changes; culminatings and declinings! Not
now, poor Paul, thou lookest wistful over the Solway
brine, by the foot of native Criffel, into blue mountainous
Cumberland, into blue Infinitude; environed with thrift,
with humble friendliness; thyself, young fool, longing
to be aloft from it, or even to be away from it. Yes,
beyond that sapphire promontory, which men name
St. Bees, which is not sapphire either, but dull sand-
stone, when one gets *close* to it, there is a world.
Which world thou shalt taste of!—From yonder White
Haven rises his smoke-clouds; ominous though in-
effectual. Proud Forth quakes at his bellying sails; had
not the wind suddenly shifted. Flamborough reapers,
home-going, pause on the hill-side; for what sulphur-
cloud is that that defaces the sleek sea; sulphur-cloud
spitting streaks of fire? A sea cockfight it is, and of the
hottest; where British *Serapis* and French-American *Bon
Homme Richard* do lash and throttle each other in their
fashion; and lo the desperate valour has suffocated the
deliberate, and Paul Jones too is of the kings of the sea.

"The Euxine, the Meotian waters felt thee next, and
long-skirted Turks, O Paul; and thy fiery soul has

wasted itself in thousand contradictions;—to no purpose.
For, in far lands, with scarlet Nassau-Siegens, with
sinful imperial Catherines, is not the heart broken, even
as at home with the mean? Poor Paul! hunger and
dispiritment track thy sinking footsteps; once or at
most twice, in this revolution-tumult, the figure of thee
emerges, mute, ghost-like, as ' with stars dim-twinkling
through.' And then, when the light is gone quite out,
a National Legislature grants ' ceremonial funeral!' As
good had been the natural Presbyterian kirk-bell, and six
feet of Scottish earth, among the dust of thy loved ones.
—*Such* world lay beyond the promontory of St. Bees."

That is at once in spirit and form a piece of poetry,
epical in the turns and diction, epical in the force
of insight and vivid brevity of presentation. A whole
history of Paul Jones lies there. Carlyle has been
smitten with sympathy for the daring adventurer, sympathy for the neglected wreck of a man and bastard
hero, and all unconsciously he writes a poem.

From his very earliest appearance as a literary man
Carlyle seemed fully conscious of his mission, and comes
before us as a reformer in his very first essay. He does
not, of course, dash out his much-needed but unpalatable
truths with the directness he afterwards does; that would
simply have frightened away review readers instead of
attracting them. He puts forward Jean Paul Richter;
and, as it were, preaches his sermon indirectly by
pleasantly telling poor Paul's changeful story. The

choice of subject not only indicates a track of reading peculiar in those days, though common enough now ; but the intense sympathy felt with the German man in his manifold struggles—the assertion of manhood against all greed and pretence—gives the key-note to his whole scheme of life and thought. Looked at with the light we can now throw upon all those early essays, we can detect the germs, the seed-grains of that great thought-tree, which has now struck so deep into English life, softly overshadowing it all. As the " music of the moon sleeps in the plain eggs of the nightingale," so we have the whole Carlyle reflected there only as through a cracked mirror (for are not all party leanings and limitations but cracks in the mirror held up to life ?) which lessened his proportions and dimmed the majesty of his presence. That of course was the necessity of review-writing while he was yet unknown ; but he uncomplainingly stooped down like a child to enter the narrow gateway and so at length came into his larger spiritual inheritance.

For Carlyle is unmistakeably a man of great presence. My readers have doubtless heard of the spirit in the legend that entered into all men's bodies and looked through their eyes. So Carlyle looks through upon us where we would but little expect to find him present. Men are quoting him when they are actually repudiating him. His kindly shadow lies over all our spiritual activity at present, giving a tone and elevation of character to it all. Alexander Smith writes a biography of Burns; so far as it professes to be original and not a mere collation of facts, it is simply a poor reflection of Carlyle's great thoughts about "our rustic bard;" George Dawson lectures cleverly and glibly: in the measure he is thinking and not merely playing with thought—he is simply alloying Carlyle's pure coin, which, like all pure gold, will not pass current in the market-place; the best moralizings of Thackeray are but applications of what often lies in one of his admired sentences from "friend Thomas;" and John Ruskin, only more honest than the rest, states plainly that he has but systematized and applied Carlyle's looser but deeper reflections. To come even to the lowest literary province; all our best leaders on America in the *Times* and otherwise during the last four years, have been but illustrations by aid of later facts of what Thomas Carlyle said nearly twenty years ago in the first of his *Latter-day Pamphlets*, titled *The Present Time.*

Severe as Carlyle is as a moralist, he is yet most tolerant of all forms of intellectual activity. He includes all and excludes none. Practically in this matter he seems to act on the axiom of Goethe—"If I call the bad *bad*, what do I gain? But if I call the good bad, I do incalculable hurt."* He borrows ideas from all depart-

---

* Even metaphysics, the most useless and empty of all forms of human knowledge, he would tolerate if it would only keep its own province, and not insist upon being the all in all of human effort and human thought.

ments, and uses them in the quaintest and most original fashion when occasion offers. His writings are thus very fertile in surprises, in illustrations that no other man ever dreamt of using. What distinguishes him from almost all our present prose writers is the intense force of individuality that will have its own way and absolutely refuses to bow to any arbitrary control whatsoever. His sentences beat with vigorous life, and are indebted for none of their force to any mere trick of words. Literature, when he entered upon it, figured itself to him as a "boundless self-devouring review," wherein as in a great seething cauldron all individuality was hopelessly swallowed up. From the very outset he raised an earnest protest against this self-sacrifice. He for one would not yield up his distinctive individuality, his character, to this Moloch of literary fashion and taste. The fault he has to find with the education in vogue is, that it sucks away this one thing that is worth the preserving, and which true education would deem it its business to preserve. Literature likewise but too truly reflects the system of education. Hence it was, perhaps, that Carlyle came to form that very unusual style both of thinking and writing which has repelled so many and even disgusted some. It may be regarded as an earnest assertion of manhood, and its rights in literature—a protest amounting to a revolt against the system of journalism, which now has imparted its spirit to the highest sections of literature—tending to cast every one into the selfsame mould, to cut down every outstanding peculiarity and round off each writer into a certain polished specimen of mediocrity; and sometimes even threatening to trim the flower of Truth itself into the chief ornamental figure in a little rhetorical *parterre*.

Carlyle has done much to bring about a revolution in these matters. A more earnest and vitalising spirit is already apparent, and is gradually descending into the lower spheres of literature. By-and-by it will leaven all, let us devoutly hope. The change will be but the visible symbol of a higher life-reform. A lesser man than Carlyle might have felt proud at the result of his teachings, which, slowly making way among the few, now indirectly and powerfully influence the many. But it is not so with him : he feels life is too earnest, and work too urgent, for his even for a moment " chewing the cud of placid reflection." Perhaps on no man has celebrity had less influence in either magnifying or impairing their real weight than on this man. He holds himself coldly apart from all touting and trumpeting; and stands on the adamantine basis of his manhood. He is perfectly self-centred. " Solid set and moulded in colossal calm," he leans not on any previous phase or school of thought or belief; and yet as I have said, all serves him, for he has mastered it all. As a man he is strictly, sternly consistent; following a great purpose with an unwavering devotion to which all obstacles ultimately yield themselves as willing vassals.

Thus a far deeper than logical unity runs through his works. A careful study shows how they gradually come to group themselves around a great principle and form one real whole. If one effort differs from another in outward aspect, it is simply because the few great guiding principles of his life (I was about to write philosophy, but forbore, fearing the word might mislead) are applied or interpreted from different stand points, and with different objects. Not but that he has been in the true sense progressive. But when one speaks of the progress of the oak, he does not mean that it has changed its distinctive character in any way, but only that it has gone on, healthily and steadily, realizing outwardly all its inward possibilities of life. It is the same with all vital growth. Hence the infinite significance of Carlyle's life to Englishmen—the far-reaching force of his teaching, and its wonderful width of application. For Carlyle's written words and his example are one, and they are properly a prophecy. What he has done and achieved each one may likewise do and attain. He is not merely a literary man; or rather, he *is* truly a literary man, in the old and better understood sense of that term when it really meant teacher and guide. He is possessed of rare and peculiar gifts; but it is not on the ground of these alone that he assumes the right to utter a word of earnest direction and warning. It is rather because he has held true to those common faculties by which men are bound together—sincerity, industry, and reverence—that he

asserts his claim to speak.   And his lesson is a grave
one, and not by any means difficult to understand when
honestly looked at.   From first to last the earnestly
inquiring soul can hear the echo of his words to the following effect :—" Oh, that each of us were true to his
possibilities, that he would once for all assure himself of
what he was sent into this strange world to be and to do,
and then set to work to realize that with such earnestness of purpose as characterized Fichte in speaking,
or Luther in fighting.   Each one is sent into this world
to make some portion of it—larger or smaller, it matters
not—somewhat more harmonious, fruitful, and beautiful,
and his whole happiness, whether he may wisely see it
or not, lies in the faithful doing of that, and of that
alone.   Every thought of man has its correspondence in
reality, in fact ; to adhere to thought only is, therefore,
to be but half faithful, nay, is to be on the road to
scepticism.   And for this simple reason, blessedness
can never lie in the perfection of man as a thinking
machine ; but rather in his practical accord with the
laws of Heaven, as written upon the face of the earth in
actual facts.   By processes of long-continued abstraction
the individual inevitably comes at length to be set in the
place of the whole universe ; disease and discord are thus
introduced, and consequently there come selfish, proud
isolation, and the neglect of those common duties by
which all men are held as in a rough bond of brotherly
union.   Act, therefore, O reader ! play thy part, whether

high or humble, like a brave noble man; and let it not concern thee at all whether men praise or condemn thy course; for, while duty still remains sacred to thee, thou art in the right way, indubitably in harmony with those powers which ever ensure victory for man, if so be he continues faithful."

So speaks Carlyle, emphatically and with such calm earnestness and intensity as are seldom met with in books. Any one may easily discover from these sentences whence arises his frank contempt for abstract theories and metaphysical speculation in its many phases; and they will even be ready, after a little reflection, perhaps, to sympathise with the doubt which frequently seems to arise upon him, whether, after all, even the loftiest thinking and writing can furnish a full sphere for true human development. With regard to the lower phases of literary endeavour, at all events, Carlyle is clearly decisive :—"Of literature," he says, "in all ways be shy rather than otherwise at present: there where thou art, work, work; whatsoever thy hand findeth to do, do it—with the hand of a man, not of a phantasm; be that thy unnoticed blessedness and exceeding great reward. Thy words, let them be few and well ordered; love silence rather than speech in these tragic days, when, for very speaking, the voice of man has fallen inarticulate to man, and hearts in this loud babbling sit dark and dumb towards one another."

Out of this feeling naturally springs his reverence

for the workers, the unconscious great ones, the few who would be true, not only as thinkers to a section of their nature, but through all force of temptation, seductions of artifice and fashion, true to the lowly relations of life as men ;—the lofty-minded toiling William Burneses; the poor, but honest, manly-hearted Johnsons; the grim - melancholy, immoveable Cromwells; the nobly-aspiring persecuted Richters; and the half-mad, fiercely-fighting Luthers attaining individual harmony through the very fire of outward discord, devilment, and vice.

That wonderful book *Sartor Resartus*, which has been read and enjoyed by hundreds who never saw clearly into its great depths, may be regarded as the short summary of Carlyle's philosophy; all his later and larger works are but as streams flowing out of it as from a reservoir, and like all streams they gradually and grandly expand as they flow, being joined by many affluents and receiving richer burdens from the regions through which they pass. And as Carlyle decisively declines to recognize any distinction between life and thought, between doing and teaching, this *Sartor Resartus* very properly takes the shape of an auto-biography. Though veiled and symbolical to a considerable degree, it is yet undoubtedly one of the truest self-revelations ever penned. It is literally quick with life. New thoughts entrance the young fresh mind as it dashes on from page to page. The force of the

writing, however, is felt to lie not in the thoughts themselves ; but in something that seems to play about them,
which, without definitely speaking itself out, takes
possession of the phantasy and the mind. Old truths
and new truths are served up together in the strangest
mélange; and ever out of the heterogeneous assort-
ment some still calm piece of nature starts forth, fixes
itself upon the eye, the heart, and resolutely refuses to
pass away from the memory. Some of the chapters
in *Sartor* literally burn themselves into the very
soul of a susceptible reader as he comes upon them
for the first time. He is whirled off into quite a new
region, and when he returns to life, half the relations
of society seem oddly changed ; but for the most part
these, as seen now, appear notwithstanding the many
abuses of them to be only the more necessary and
venerable.

The first dip into *Sartor* has the effect of an electric
shock. It is a short time before its influence in bracing
up the spiritual system and sharpening the insight, is
evident. Self-renunciation is the bourne to which it
constantly points. Everywhere it pulses with the movement of blood as in a warrior's veins on the eve of
battle. It is, in fact, a piece of nature this *Sartor*, at
once great, rude, and beautiful; redolent with wisdom
also, it buds out on all sides into rich practical suggestions. Doubts and fears we see fly away into
the distance when man rushes bravely into the fight;

in other words, when the facts of life are faithfully and boldly faced. It is a calm prophecy of freedom to the heavy-laden, sore-beaten ones, whether they are toiling for the " daily bread," or for the yet nobler heritage, the " bread of life." All in the first few chapters has the sweet soft flush of a summer idyll; then suddenly come storm, tumult, and disorder, the storm not for long being relieved even by the wild gleams of light that dash from time to time across the world of the mind; but calmly the day at last melts into a still eventide, and all closes in peace, repose, and tranquil blessedness of dutiful working. In the " Everlasting Yea" lies the root of all *manlike* attainment. After much wrestle the secret has been caught, the author has himself conquered that which is false, partial, outward, circumstantial; lives in the will alone, and by the will gets sure and permanent footing in the whole, the true, the eternal.

It is a circumstance not without significance that in the later edition of Carlyle's works, *Sartor Resartus* and the " Hero-worship " should have been bound up together. For different as they appear in outward form, they are closely related in spirit and purpose. More than any other of his books, the Lectures on Heroes has its direct root in *Sartor*. It is the developement of the main stream of thought into definite historical ground. While the principle was dealt with simply as such in *Sartor* and elsewhere, to the casual reader it seemed constantly as if threatening to dissipate itself, like some Eastern streams, in dry sand. But here, to carry out the figure, it flows on, a fruitful river, refreshing and beautifying a wide track of landscape, partially known to us. Any one who reads carefully the chapter towards the end of *Sartor*, titled " Organic Filaments," (a most significant and suggestive heading, by the way,) will at once see the relation in which Hero-worship stands to the earlier work—as full-flower to the bud, to put it shortly. In the Hero-worship our author seems to say, " Here, I present you with some great principles, which you must be pleased to accept as to what heroes are, and the part they play in human history. But I do not ask you to receive my examples or types as perfect ones, by any means. They are defective all ; very imperfect some of them, and only in a dim, far-off way indicate my meaning. I was not free to use some types, for altogether sacred reasons, and I rejected others, which would have better suited my purpose than those chosen, simply because they were not so well known to you. But yet you will please to recollect that these are realities, and not fictions, I have dealt with, and as such they will surely serve a certain purpose—to temper the light, that you may apprehend it the easier and better. For had I been bold enough to have chosen higher specimens, the result would have been to confuse you yet more than I am likely to do. But pray do not puzzle yourselves too much about certain historical individuals such as my position has here compelled me to choose for illustration, nor about single actions, nor special points of character; the great principles are such as can be seized upon and appropriated quite independently of these. Odin, Mahomet, Napoleon, and the rest are, in fact, but ragged figures placed between you and the glory of eternal truths, manifesting themselves throughout all human history, and while they reflect so much of the light as may help any earnest inquiring soul to clearer convictions as to life, and a truer basis of faith as a really vital thing, they serve also to qualify the strange brightness of such truths at first, and to keep it from hurting or dazzling weak eyes. For to show you the whole of the light in words, or in any such way, were impossible, and yet that light itself may be struck out of every heart, even the lowliest now before me."

The root principle of hero-worship is very clearly enunciated in this passage from *Past and Present :*— " My brother, the brave man has to give his life away. Give it, I advise thee ;—thou dost not expect to *sell* thy life in any adequate manner ? What price, for example, would content thee ? The just price of thy LIFE to thee, —why God's entire Creation to thyself, the whole universe of Space, the whole eternity of Time, and what they hold ; that is the price that would content thee ; that, and if thou wilt be candid, nothing short of that ! It is thy all; and for it thou wouldst have all. Thou art an unreasonable mortal;—or rather thou art a poor *infinite* mortal, who in thy narrow clay prison here *seemest* so unreasonable! Thou wilt never sell thy Life, or any part of thy Life in a satisfactory manner. Give it, like a royal heart; let the price be nothing; thou hast then in a certain sense got *All* for it! The heroic man,—and is not every man, God be thanked, a potential hero?— has to do so in all times and circumstances. In the most heroic age as in the most unheroic, he will have to say, as Burns said proudly and humbly of his little Scottish songs, little dew-drops of Celestial Melody in an age when so much was unmelodious:—'By Heaven, they shall either be invaluable or of no value: I do not need your guineas for them!' It is an element which should and must enter deeply into all settlements of wages here below. They never will be 'satisfactory' otherwise; they cannot, O Mammon Gospel, they never can! Money for my little piece of work—'to the extent that will allow me to keep on working;' yes this,—unless you mean that I shall go my ways before the work is all taken out of me. But as to wages—!"

Here we have the central idea of the Hero-worship quite relieved from confusion with any arbitrary historical type it may be illustrated by; and I have now simply to ask whether that does not sound very like a reiteration in language really fitted to the time, of the very first principles of Christian teaching?

To those who have formed their notion of Carlyle, not for themselves, from a careful and unprejudiced study of his writings, but from reviews in newspapers or semi-religious magazines, it will most assuredly seem strange enough for me here and now to declare, emphatically and with the utmost seriousness, that Carlyle's Hero-worship is essentially an assertion of the *might of Humility*. This I do advisedly, however; and fully cognizant of the loud outcry that has been raised about worship of intellect and of sheer brute force, &c. Such charges are easily raised, and have been raised again and again against men of the most devout character; but never, I believe, with so little reason and with so much blindness as against Thomas Carlyle. I can almost fancy I hear him answer—not with contempt, but rather with the " wise indifference of the wise "—in some such words as these:—" Intellect, great will, brute Force ! What are these compared with the unconscious power of lowly wisdom? or what their results compared with its silent but enduring triumphs? Even the ancients knew better than to worship the like of these you name, unless closely identified with and even subdued by other and loftier qualities ! Hercules had gone through twelve labours, I believe, not alone for his own benefit either, and had denied himself in innumerable ways before even the Greeks made of him a hero ! Wisdom is the one enduring power of this world, because this world was

made by a wise and just God. The root of wisdom is
humility. To *do* justice is the best way to fight for it,
and that is by no means easy; nay, it is of all things
difficult: and the man who against all temptations will
persist in that must have learned the grandest, wisest of
life-lessons—to rank his own claims and rights as zero
compared with the claims and the rights which God,
the universe, and humanity have over him. ' For
who if he had even his rights would escape a sore
whipping?' To be wholly unconscious of rights and
claims is to be a hero. And so humility thus comes
literally to rule the world; and, as I construe it, all
right Christianity enforces this same humility as its
first and fundamental requirement. And so also is it
in my scheme of things; the principle not so very
difficult either to disentangle from the loose and rugged
manner in which the half-blind, artificial, down-rushing
age has compelled me to speak. Here, for instance, is
a passage written now many years ago, but which I
assert holds the leading principle in all the attempts
I make to get at the meanings of man's life and men's
life—to eliminate truth from error—to separate the
little grain of wheat from the abundant chaff of History:

" Of conquest we may say that it never yet went by
brute force and compulsion; conquest of that kind does
not endure. Conquest, along with power of compulsion,
an essential universally in human society, must bring
benefit along with it, or men, of the ordinary strength

of men, will fling it out. The strong man, what is he if we will consider? The wise man; the man with the gift of method, of faithfulness and valour, all of which are of the basis of wisdom; who has insight into what is what, into what will follow out of what, the eye to see and the hand to do; who is *fit* to administer, to direct and *guidingly* command: he is the strong man. His muscles and bones are no stronger than ours; but his soul is stronger, his soul is wiser, clearer,—is better and nobler, for that is, has been, and ever will be the root of all clearness worthy of such a name. . . . . It is the heart that sees before the head *can* see; let us know that; and know, therefore, that the Good alone is deathless and victorious; that Hope is sure and steadfast in all phases of this 'Place of Hope.'—Shiftiness, quirk, attorney-cunning, is a thing that fancies itself, and is often fancied to be, talent; but it is luckily mistaken in that. Succeed truly it does, what is called succeeding; and even must in general succeed if the dispensers of success be of due stupidity: men of due stupidity will needs say to it, ' *Thou* art wisdom, rule thou!' Whereupon it rules. But Nature answers, ' No, this ruling of thine is not according to *my* laws : thy wisdom was not wise enough! Dost thou take me too for a quackery, for a conventionality, and attorneyism? This chaff that thou sowest into my bosom, though it pass at the poll-booth and elsewhere for seed-corn, *I* will not grow wheat out of it, for it is chaff!' "

And, continuing, he would say—"This other short passage may be taken by each one as 'practical application' of the above, or recipe for becoming fit to really rule :—It is written, 'seekest thou great things, seek them not;' live where thou art, only live wisely, live diligently. . . . For the working of the good and brave, seen or unseen, endures literally forever and cannot die. Is a thing nothing because the Morning Papers have not mentioned it? Or can a nothing be made something by never so much babbling of it there? Far better that no morning or evening newspaper mentioned it; that the right hand knew not what the left was doing! Literature is great. And yet, what of books? Hast thou not already a Bible to write and publish in print that is eternal ; namely, a life to lead? Silence, too, is great ; there should be great silent ones too."

Carlyle's faith is large in the vital force of individual good-doing. As the little pebble dropt into the expansive lake pulses the whole fluid mass into a new relation, and makes it seek a new level; so is it with noble human actions. Their influence upon the world is as sure as that of gravitation upon the body we throw upward. True lives, let them be never so humble, are like rivulets running underground, making the earth green ; pure so long as they flow unnoticed onwards, getting defiled and muddy at bottom as soon as they emerge into open day, and become great deep wells and tarns. These are but the visible results or symbols of much vital but invisible worth, which too, in the very fact of becoming visible, has lost much of its secret fertilizing power. Burns is the outcome of many generations such as that heroic father of his; Luther is a well into which many secret and blessed veinlets have run; and Mirabeau concentrates in himself the forgotten fiery virtues of his ancestry, which reappear and exhaust themselves in him owing to the. terrible infusion of moral mud. Thus true-living triumphs over time, finding at length visible outgrowths. These outgrowths are the forces men can lay hold upon and appreciate, and as such Carlyle uses them for the illustration of principles which yet always remove themselves away from the region of recognition and historical fact, into that of the silent work and suffering which precedes history, and in fact, first of all makes it possible. The acorn has a sore fight of it, we may be sure, amid the dank darkness and decay under the soil, before it comes forth a tree on which men can gaze for centuries with delight. And so it is with History. "The flocking and fighting of kites and crows, is the history of the Heptarchy," says Milton. Another replies: "Obscure fighting of kites and crows was not the history of it; but was only what the dim historians of it saw right to record. Were not forests quietly felled, bogs drained, fields made arable, towns built, laws made, and the thought and practice of men in many ways perfected? Or was the smith idle or hammering only war-tools; he had. learned metallurgy, stithy work in general; and made ploughshares withal, and adzes and hammers." In this way Carlyle constantly dives beneath the historical to a deeper which underlies it; proclaiming ever and anon definitely enough, that his greatest heroes of all are the silent ones, of whom history has failed to tell us, and who doubtless realized in their peaceful yet painfully-struggling lives that latest of the Christian beatitudes—" Blessed are the humble, are they that are *not* known." It is a principle this, around which of necessity must gather pious reverence and high human hopes; and it is constantly enunciated by Carlyle, with the utmost decision and clearness. It is, indeed, the central idea of his writings; "the main haunt and region of his song," as poet Wordsworth phrased it. This constant undercurrent reference to the "great silent ones," gives a purity, a beauty, and a reverent worth to all he has written, sweetly and softly relieving it even when he *appears* to get intoxicated with some form of historic greatness. For ever and anon he turns regretfully away even from a Burns or a Goethe, to refresh his soul by silent communion with that still victorious brotherhood. If there is one article of the creed Carlyle has no doubt whatever about, it is that one which asserts "a communion of saints."

To my thinking, the very finest passage in Carlyle's writings, occurs in one of his latest essays. It is a fine illustration and proof of what has just been said,—affording a clear inlet into the character of the man, and his way of interpreting history, which with him, since he sets so much value upon the select few brave, faithful, individual lives, properly resolves itself into biography. Thus then he closes his estimate of Rahel Varnhagen Von Ense—that strange woman, "equal to the highest thoughts of her century," and yet whose duty it was, " not to write or to act, but only to live :—"

"Beautiful it is to see and understand that no worth, known or unknown, can die even in this earth. The work an unknown good man has done is like a vein of water flowing hidden underground, secretly making the ground green ; it flows and flows, it joins itself with other veins and veinlets ; one day it will start forth as a visible perennial well. Ten dumb centuries had made the speaking Dante ; a well he of many veinlets. William Burnes or Burns was a poor peasant ; could not prosper in ' his seven acres of nursery-ground,' nor any enter- prise of trade and toil ; had to ' thole a factor's snash,' and read attorney-letters in his poor hut, ' which threw us all into tears,' a man of no money capital at all, of no account at all ; yet a brave man, a wise, and just ; in evil fortune faithful, unconquerable to the death. And there wept withal among the others, a boy named *Robert*, with a heart of melting pity, of greatness and fiery wrath ; and *his* voice, *fashioned here by this poor father*, does it not already reach, like a great elegy, like a stern prophecy, to the ends of the world ? ' Let me make the songs, and you shall make the laws !' What chan -

cellor, king, senator, begirt with never such sumptuosity, dyed velvet, blaring and celebrity, could you have named in England, that was so momentous as that William Burns? Courage!—"

Secret self-denying action is, according to Carlyle the hidden root, out of which springs that mystic union of man with man which ultimately comes to form the basis and ground of continuance of all laws and social arrangements whatsoever. The hero's mission is to promote and in all ways establish that union by the recommendation of self-denial and the practice of it in his own life. This idea gives the point of contact between Carlyle's hero-worship and his political economy as enunciated in *Chartism, Past and Present*, and the *Latter-day Pamphlets*, which books any really open-minded thoughtful soul will find are nothing else than the application of the loftiest Christian principles to the every-day concerns of men and the vital questions of the period. The foundation of the State, as of the Church, is traceable to this principle of self-denial, whose first practical utterance will be a revolt against the half-heathen *dicta*, that in these later times have been imported into political economy. The State is not essentially separated from the Church, nor opposed to it. They are one, rest on the spiritual, and derive their vitality from it; and for their successful upbuilding both alike demand the exercise of strong faith. Hence Carlyle's religion will not express itself in abstract formulas or articles.

Only one sphere he regards as the fitting embodiment
of the religious idea, and that is the practical relations.
A religion which refuses to make these its symbols and
its fitting channels of expression is fruitless, hollow, and
on the way to being wholly false, if not already so. He
approaches all secular questions from the sacred side—
carries into the political sphere quite an unusual element,
which yet is by no means new. He deals in the most
paradoxical and contemptuous way with the doctrines
embodied in such dogmas as "Buy in the cheapest
market and sell in the dearest," and a "fair day's wages
for a fair day's work." Not but that Carlyle recognizes
clearly enough the fact that "man must live by bread."
He has as clear practical views on that side the question
as any who have written on it; but he never for a
moment forgets in his political economy that "man
lives not by bread alone." That is his peculiarity; and
it is the perpetual presence of that element with him
which exalts him to the level of a religious teacher.
The exclusion from the domain of political economy of
that one element by which man becomes really man, and
linked at once to a Past and a Future, is with Carlyle a
sin and the parent of many sins, practically fruitful of
evil in every walk of life—from the puffery, the cheating,
and the division of interests so apparent everywhere, up
to the startling phenomena of Peterloos and French
Revolutions. His theory of values is a rather peculiar
one,—not at all likely to be accepted by the gentlemen

who write clever "money articles," for the daily prints. It so abruptly resolves all value into the question of the quantity of *valour*, virtue, heroism, developed as it were by means of these others. Means and ends are so suddenly reversed by Carlyle that the disciples of Bentham on reading him may well doubt if they have not got into another world. What value attaches to anything is with him ultimately determined by the measure of that other quite intangible and spiritual quality which it may have been the means of maintaining. "My friend, brag not yet of our American cousins! Their quantity of cotton, dollars, industry and resources, I believe to be almost unspeakable; but I can by no means worship the like of these. What great human soul, what great thought, what great noble thing that one could worship, or loyally admire, has yet been produced there? None, the American cousins have yet done none of these things." Trade becomes mere "Beaverism," — a horrible self-devouring monster, though it may not know it, when no vein of the other and higher runs through it. Society on such a basis of mere deception and insatiable greed cannot long maintain its equilibrium. Hence come crises, American civil wars, revolutions, to show that all is not so secure as men persuaded themselves it was; and even by such rude means, in default of a better, more peaceful way, to bear in on their minds the fact of a Higher, force a glimpse of it upon them, as the curtains of custom and order and rule are for a moment rent asunder before their wondering gaze. As with values so with wages. Carlyle holds that no really honest piece of work was ever yet done towards the doing of which there went not elements that could not be paid for in money. For the honest worker literally gives himself in his work, be it high or low, stamps his character upon it, and sends it abroad a witness to the might of goodness; and every man who looks upon it afterwards will declare it a beautiful and reverent thing.

And thus we are justifiably led to look on Carlyle's various books as being simply separate chapters on Hero-worship, for all are but recipes for the practice of goodness and recommendations of true heroism. Good men, according to him, are the "welling fountain-heads" of progress; all true progress being but the disentanglement of the inner element of light and truth, so that it may also become supreme in outward and visible fact. Each new development is an additional treasure to the race, and can never again perish. In the life of each virtuous man something is thus gained for society and the universe. For, as no man can possibly live isolated, the good man becomes the centre of living influences which diffuse themselves over a far broader area than mortal mind can conceive. By a necessity of his nature he seeks to join himself with others of like spirit, and these in their union form the only real available working church in the world.

Out of *their* hearts very literally are the issues of life. They are the links, which in all ages have held society in contact with those eternal realities typed in the uncouth phrases so frequently used by Carlyle—the "Eternities" and the "Silences," which words are chosen chiefly for their very rudeness of look, as rugged finger-posts to point us back to that side of human affairs, consideration of which is so very apt to be lost sight of when new arrangements are made and new relations entered into. And through those unknown, pious, devout souls, though the mass of men have never practically believed it, a thousand unseen rills pour continuously their sweet waters into the bitter sea of human history, which without such would become inevitably a dead sea covering only other Gomorrahs. Therefore, eloquently writes Carlyle,—" For properly as many men as there are in a nation who *can* withal see Heaven's *invisible* justice, and know it to be on earth also omnipotent ; so many men are there who stand between a nation and perdition." And again :—" Beyond doubt the Almighty Maker made this England too ; and has been and for ever is miraculously present here. The more is the pity for us if our eyes are grown owlish, and cannot see this fact of facts when it is before us ! Once it was well known that the Highest did of a surety dwell in this nation, divinely avenging, and divinely saving and rewarding ; leading by steep and flaming paths, by heroisms, pieties, and noble acts and thoughts, this nation heavenward, if it would and dared. Known or not, this (or else the terrible inverse of this) is for evermore the fact! The History of England, had the fine or other arts taught us to read it aright, is the record of the divine appearances among us; of the brightnesses out of Heaven that have irradiated our terrestrial struggle; and spanned our wild deluges and weltering seas of trouble as with celestial rainbows and symbols of eternal covenants." . . . . " Nor, deeply as the fact is now forgotten, has it essentially in the smallest degree ceased to be the fact, nor will it cease. With every nation it is so, and with every man—for every nation, I suppose, was made by God, and every man too? Only there are some nations, like some men, who know it: and some who do not. The great men and nations are they that have known it well; the small and contemptible of men and nations are they that have either never known it, or soon forgotten it, and never laid it to heart. Of these comes nothing. The measure of a nation's greatness, of its worth under the sky to God and to man, is not the quantity of bullion it has realized, but the quantity of heroisms it has achieved, of noble pieties and valiant wisdoms that were in it— that still are in it."

That man is victor over " Circumstance" or Fate in all forms and phases of it is one of Carlyle's favourite themes. He rejoices that there is a region, and that too the only vital sphere of man's influence on which he is indeed supreme, and the accomplishment of his whole being therein, no one—man or devil—can prevent, if so be the man is true, through all opposition and temptation, to his aspirations and hopes. The individual is all—the environment is nothing. "Yes, reader; all this thou hast heard about 'force of circumstances,' 'the creature of the time," 'balancing of motives,' and who knows what melancholy stuff to the like purport, wherein thou, as in a nightmare dream, sittest paralysed and hast no force left,—was in very truth, if Johnson and waking men are to be credited, little other than a hag-ridden vision of death-sleep; some *half-fact*, more fatal at times than a whole falsehood. Shake it off; awake; up and be doing, even as it is given thee!" It is the spirit in which a man lives and works that makes him heroic or unheroic. The element he deals with is but the medium which may either help or hinder his true development. Action—earnest, productive action is the clearing away of mists and impediments from the soul. Carlyle consequently admires vigorous action, though it may not be devoted to what are usually recognised as lofty ends: the humblest piece of work, if done honestly, he accepts as a sort of victory, and the beginning of still greater victories, because this is the first, though lowest form, in which human freedom must be asserted. For "work is of a religious nature:"—work is of a brave nature, which it is the aim of all religion to be. All work of man is as the swimmer's: a waste ocean (of circumstance) threatens to devour him; if he front it not bravely, it will keep its word. By incessant wise defiance of it, lusty rebuke and buffet of it, behold how it loyally supports him— bears him as its conqueror along. " It is so," says Goethe, " with all things man undertakes in this world." But viewed as a matter of high moral and spiritual influence, man's actions are of wonderful significance. There is no true teaching apart from living and example: therefore would Carlyle have truth, honestly applied on a low practical sphere of daily action, rather than the very loftiest of abstract and theoretical preachifyings. " Knowledge," says he, " the knowledge that will hold good in working, cleave thou to that: for nature herself accredits that—says yea to that. Properly thou hast no other knowledge but what thou hast got by working: the rest is yet all a hypothesis of knowledge; a thing to be argued of in schools, a thing floating in the clouds, in endless logic-vortices till we try it and fix it. ' Doubt of whatever kind can be ended by action alone.'"

This assertion of man's complete independence of everything outward and circumstantial, and the victory which the true man can accomplish within himself, whatever may be his condition, gives rise to two ideas which have proved a puzzle to some readers. Carlyle defines injustice as an " acted lie;" declares it a nothing, an abortion; doomed by the very nature of it

to failure and ultimate destruction, and yet his protest
against it rises sometimes to so high a key, that it
might not unreasonably be construed into a defence of
revolution. Then on the very next page he is warmly
advocating permanence in all the social relations.
Contradictory as these ideas might seem at first sight,
they are but sides of the same deep-settled conviction.
Injustice is self-destructive ; its victories are only apparent, temporary, deceptive ; it is neutralized and
defeated in its out-go every day by the deeds of the free
and the true of men. Silent submission under wrong,
deeply felt to be a wrong, is essentially an overcoming
of it. Ten unknown righteous men, could they have
been found, would have saved Sodom—that is, would
have made united life still possible there, even under
the false conditions it had reached, by constantly pouring
into the moral desert an unseen force of truth and
virtue. When men need to take up arms to forcibly
destroy a form of evil, it is a proof that they too have
come to live in the outward : had they not done so they
would have triumphed even on earth by faith,—by
the might of their simple silent well-doing. For no
true victory over wrong, but only new and bitter crops
of wrongs, could by possibility come of opposing force
to force for ends which are moral. When revolution,
fearful, bloody, does begin, it is a proof that the nation
has lost its saviours—the " great silent ones," according
to Carlyle—a proof that there is no longer the minimum

of heroic lives in the nation to save it by the truer and everyway more glorious method. In this respect, as in some others, it may be said, " Blessed are the people whose annals are vacant." For when such secret good men can no longer be found, society has lost its true basis, and, like a pyramid on a shifting quicksand, it must reel and fall. Revolutions are of use to purify by destroying the material elements in which men had come solely to trust ; to revive faith in goodness and in the unseen, which, after all, are really but figures of the same thing. Permanence, therefore, according to Carlyle, means that settledness of life and aim, which springs from a regenerated life, and which finds in the faithful and earnest fulfilment of duty an abundant reward ; sufficient to itself it can accept without regret or desire the place assigned to it by Providence, and say in genuine faith : "Here is my America, or nowhere." "Here am I placed to be a centre of fruitfulness, order, and harmony."

And thus significantly writes Carlyle :—" Oh, unwise mortals that for ever change and shift, and say, Yonder, not Here ! Wealth richer than both the Indies lies everywhere for man, if he will endure. Not his oaks only and his fruit trees, his very heart roots itself wherever he will abide ;—roots itself, draws nourishment from the deep fountains of Universal Being ! Vagrant Sam Slicks, who rove over the earth, doing ' strokes of business,' what wealth have they ? Horseloads, shiploads, of white or yellow metal: in very sooth, what *are* these? Slick rests nowhere, he is homeless. He can build stone or marble houses; but to continue in them is denied him. The wealth of a man is the number of things which he loves and blesses, which he is loved and blessed by! The herdsman in his poor clay shealing, where his very cow and dog are friends to him, and not a cataract but carries memories for him, and not a mountain-top but nods old recognition: his life all encircled as in blessed mother's arms, is it poorer than Slick's with the ass-loads of yellow metal on his back? Unhappy Slick! Alas, there has so much grown nomadic, ape-like, with us; so much will have, with whatever pain, repugnance, and 'impossibility' to alter itself, to fix itself again,— in some wise way, *in any not delirious way!* "

These few sentences again show the idea on the other side :—" No man is justified in resisting, by word or deed, the authority he lives under for a light cause, be such authority what it may. Obedience, little as many may consider that side of the matter, is the primary duty of man. No man but is bound indefeasibly, with all force of obligation, to obey. Parents, teachers, superiors, leaders: these all creatures recognize as deserving obedience. . . . . Rebel, without due and most due cause, is the ugliest of words; the first rebel was Satan."

Everything in Carlyle's scheme thus seems to resolve

itself ultimately into individual goodness, and to play around that as round a vital centre. Apart from that there is nothing permanent, or worthy, or beautiful. True wealth lies therein, and all other sort of wealth is strictly conditioned by its presence. Progress, reform, poetries, fine arts, all take their rise here so far as they are real and fruitful, and not shows merely, empty, idle, and in spirit false. " The inmost becomes in due time the outmost," says Emerson. All that is hidden shall be made manifest, is averred by a still higher authority. It is a Christian faith alone which could utter itself in such words as these :—" No worth, known or unknown, *can* die even in this earth." Of a truth, its destiny is to be found many days after it was sown, bearing fruit to gladden and to bless men's hearts. Out of this spirit of serene faith, Carlyle can write for our refreshment such triumphantly hopeful words as these :—" How else is a moral reform to be looked for but in this way, that more and more good men are, by a bountiful Providence, sent hither to dis-seminate Goodness : literally to *sow* it, as in seeds shaken abroad by the living tree ? For such, in all ages and places, is the nature of a good man ; he is ever a mystic creative centre of goodness : his influence, if we con-sider it, is not to be measured ; for his works do not die, but being of Eternity, are eternal, and in new transformation, and ever wider diffusion, endure, living and life-giving. Thou who exclaimest over the horrors and baseness of the Time, and how Diogenes would now need *two* lanterns in daylight, think of this : over the Time thou hast no power ; to redeem a World sunk in dishonesty has not been given thee : solely over one man therein thou hast quite absolute uncontrollable power ; him redeem, him make honest ; it will be something, it will be much, and thy life and labour not in vain." . . . . " For what is the meaning of nobleness, if this be not noble ? In a valiant suffering for others, not in a slothful making others suffer for us, did nobleness ever lie. The chief of men is he who stands in the van ; fronting the peril which frightens back all others ; which, if it be not vanquished, will devour the others. Every noble crown is, and on earth will for ever be, a crown of thorns."

In the light of Christianity such statements should by no means be regarded as strange or startling. They are old Christian truths, once regarded as common because they were vital, and here have a look of novelty because they have been practically forgotten—become old-world words if anything, and surprise us when re-stated with vital force and in a form adapted to the day we live in.

It must be admitted, however, that in the attempt to resolve Carlyle's system into a single root in the simple assertion of the indestructibility and victorious nature of goodness—some difficulties present themselves, arising from the manner in which he has dealt with history, and the arbitrary types he has chosen

to illustrate his Hero-worship by. To the genuine
student of Carlyle this point, after all, would not be
very hard of explanation. I shall, however, devote
some pages to show the relation of history so-called
to Carlyle's scheme of heroes, as it is not unlikely that
this essay may fall into the hands of some persons who
have not had an opportunity of making acquaintance
with him. It must be borne in mind, then, that Carlyle does not by any means express himself absolutely
satisfied with many of his hero-types. The defects
and necessities of history alone have forced him to
adopt them, and thus we cannot read the Hero-worship
long with any degree of thought, till we are directly
referred back to what has been from the first—or at all
events from the date of that remarkable essay on " Characteristics"—a great point with him,—the distinction
namely between the Conscious and the Unconscious in
history and human life. Here, if we examine well, we
will find the key to many perplexing questions which
may arise. That Carlyle seeks so keenly to distinguish
on all occasions between the Conscious and the Unconscious is the ground at once of his quarrel with
history as it has for most part been written hitherto,
and his marked joy over the " veridical" in reference
even to what might seem to others wholly unimportant.
It is the ground, too, of the contradiction which from
first to last is observed on close examination to run
through the Hero-worship. The blundering, lumbering

records of vicious courts delight not him, nor the red-tape lists of state pageantries and pitched battles : he turns away from these with a sigh to gloat over the little unartistic notes of a Boswell, who has laid hold of an unconscious hero and true worker, and clung to him firmly through good report and through bad report. " The great is vital, and knows not that it is great," is his constant maxim. In the measure it becomes historical, so does it compromise its true character. For history, properly taken, is the record of the little, the conscious, the diseased. But yet those disruptive forces history deals with are firmly held together in a great mysterious law of order which is constantly evolving new forces out of the death of old forms of life. That deep, silent, reconstructive process, in which the lives of good men hold such an all-important place, is not, or has not, to the full been recognized by historians. They have failed to seize hold on that one element from which all history derives its significance, and in which all the different parts of history, however opposed to each other in outward character and seeming, centre and are reconciled. Carlyle's Hero-worship, then, may be regarded as an endeavour to find a more vital root for historical phenomena—an attempt, in a rude, suggestive, disconnected way, to link the seen and visible with a secret invisible sphere on which the other is constantly dependent ; and, by this means to recall men once more to a vital faith. In the indestructible and eternal nature of good or of duty, Carlyle, as I have said, finds this root principle. It is the silver thread this, which runs through all the annals, bringing the ancient and the modern together—drawing heathen and Christian, near and remote, under one benign law of progress. The poor black woman who showed such kindness to over-wearied hungry Mungo Park is a lady (*hlafdig*, loaf-giveress) and a heroine— a sister to all the great ones of the earth. As our mighty rivers on whose bosoms fleets float safely lose themselves in the distant mountain ranges, so all historic phenomena that is really worthy derives its greatness from elements which directly relate themselves to the secret and holy in the lives of unknown men.

So it comes that in the very measure individual heroes have become historical, does Carlyle feel free to deal with them. That very consciousness of their heroism which mostly had the power to push them into high places makes them all the less sacred and un-approachable to him. As they seem to grow great from the human side so they decline from the divine, just as no object can cast its shadow on both sides at once. And Carlyle is rigidly consistent. He tells us frankly, for instance, that Mahomet was not chosen as the best or greatest type of the hero-prophet, but simply because he was most historical—the one " we are freest to speak of." The measure of our right to speak of anything is in a ratio with the degree in which it has spoken of

itself and proclaimed itself, or got itself proclaimed, which ultimately is about the same thing. For this reason, says Carlyle again, and not without meaning :— " The greatest of all heroes is one whom we name not here! Let sacred silence meditate that sacred matter; you will find it the *ultimate* perfection of a principle extant throughout man's whole history on earth." *
Instead of his choosing to speak of David, or Moses, or Solomon, or the Apostles, he selects modern names mostly, of poets, fighters, legislators; but we are not on that account to conclude that the Scripture heroes are to be ranked lower because they are not spoken of; rather we should rank them the very higher on that simple account.

But it must be admitted that men are peculiar and unaccountable mixtures. Their lives will not square themselves off into mechanical precision at any time or in any circumstances, but are full of contradictions and puzzles from first to last. Even into the lowest, enlightening and beautifying it, the higher may shine as through some chance cranny. For no man lives but has possibilities of greatness in him, and that because he has possibilities of goodness. " Brother, thou hast possibility in thee for much : the possibility of writing on the eternal skies the record of a heroic life." " Absolutely without originality there is no man." " Is not every man, God be thanked, a potential hero ?" asks

---

* The reader is referred to Addenda, " Historical Christianity," p. 243.

Carlyle again. Of the few good lines in Bailey's *Festus* the following are among the best, and have a reference to the point here treated of :—

> Laws there are
> Twain in the which man walks ; the law of law,
> Of chance and custom, creed, time, circumstance—
> Law superficial this ; the other is
> To those which breathe the light, the law of laws,
> Eternal, spiritual, central. These to mix
> Breeds chaos, and yet not to mix
> Impossible to cultivated man.

The deep and the superficial,—the vital and the dead, the conscious and the unconscious, do run strangely together in man's, and in men's experience ! The two conflicting elements get so mixed up that it is of all things difficult to say often of a special result, whether it comes of the one or the other, or in what measure it owes its origin to each. To tell the ring of the true coin is a merit; and a great advantage would be conferred by the man who would give us a simple recipe for detecting it. Generally speaking, history only " makes confusion worse confounded." It mingles quackery and sincerity—the conscious and the unconscious—in an interminable jumble, and adopts quite an artificial and arbitrary method of marking off and distinguishing. The very Devil, when he gets rid of his hoofs, horns, and tail, and cleverly plays the Tory, will be great if not divine with Alison and that class, and when he turns Whig again he will be bepraised and bespattered by the whole tribe of Macaulays and Russells. Hence it is that not only in actual life but even towards the dead we do quite mistaken obeisance, by too implicitly receiving the verdicts of history, sometimes abnegating even what " The Book " has taught us.

It is quite true, at the same time, that we need not seek for perfect men. As it was by a rent that the inner glory of the Temple was revealed to the people of old, so will it ever be in the history of great men. Were it not for the rents in them,—their weaknesses, or errors— their glory would never break through upon us ; it would be but as vague colourless beams of white light. David could not have sung such Psalms as those unless he had so sadly sinned and fallen. The first Adam's disobedience and the second Adam's triumph are realized over again in the lives of all who are true and brave. So we need not seek for perfect men in any abstract theoretical sense whatever. Life or history knows them not. We must first worm out of the Sphinx her secret, and then apply it to see who of those who have gone before us are worthy. So we will justly absolve or condemn ; so give entrance or refuse it to those who seek admittance into our Pantheon. And as has already been said, even the worst of men have not only possibilities to lay hold upon the Highest, but must in some remote degree have developed these, in order even to prevent life becoming insupportably miserable ; so we must be generous to others while struggling to be true to ourselves.

That Carlyle annihilates the very types he has set up to temporarily teach by is significant and suggestive of much. From a logical point of view he seems indeed to contradict himself sadly with regard to them. But the reason is simply that some of them have pretty distinctive relations both to the Conscious and Unconscious —have in their lives strangely mixed up the two laws which poet Bailey refers to. Mahomet is very conscious of one phase of his greatness, and out of that sprung, as by necessity, his errors, his stupidities, his sensualisms, and also his large historical self-assertion, if one might name it so. But he also held unconsciously of the deeper, the silent, and lived or testified to far greater truths than he even proclaimed or was in any way conscious of.

There is, for instance, the altogether important fact, that for the first fifty years of his life, in the very midst of sensualism, sanctioned, too, by religion, Mahomet lived a pure, upright, busy, earnest, beautiful life; in the very heat of his years yielding to no vice, remaining faithful, tenderly faithful to his Kadijah, and loved by those around and under him. That circumstance, too, is noted by Carlyle with satisfaction. Perhaps this is the vital *unconscious* fact in Mahomet's history *for us;* which constitutes him a sort of humble hero, and an exemplar which we, too, are bound to follow so far as it goes; for by this life of his, Mahomet wedded himself to the sacred and inexhaustible, more than by any spoken words whatever. Nature endures some divergence from her laws, if there are approximations, compensating somewhat on other sides; but if a man comes to live wholly and solely in the false, the superficial, the circumstantial, then she rejects him, and at last scourges him as with scorpions. Mahomet managed to the end to keep some slight hold on the real; influences from that early silent, dutiful life of his, well up, and are a light to him which flickers and sinks sometimes, but ever rises again and goes not totally out. And so it is that he keeps hold on men's memories so long.

Carlyle speaks of Mahomet almost in one breath as having been at once true and false. He was both; it depends entirely on the side from which he is viewed. Did he not bring light to the Arabs in doing away with idolatry, and proclaiming the law of complete *submission* to Allah? Yes; but he erred and brought confusion by choosing the sword, and by writing a cumbrous self-conscious Koran. Thus Carlyle can say, and quite consistently, of Mahomet, when treating of the calm unconscious Shakspeare as hero-poet : — " And, at bottom, was it not perhaps far better that this Shakspeare, every way an unconscious man, was *conscious* of no heavenly message. He did not feel, like Mahomet, because he saw into these internal splendours, that he specially was the ' prophet of God;' and was he not greater than Mahomet in that? Greater, and also, if we compute strictly, as we did in Dante's case, more

successful. It was intrinsically an error, that notion of
Mahomet's of his supreme prophethood; and has come
down to us inextricably involved in error to this day:
dragging along with it such a coil of fables, impurities,
intolerances, as makes it a questionable step for me here
and now to say as I have done, that Mahomet was a true
speaker, and not rather an ambitious charlatan, per-
versity and simulacrum—no speaker, but a babbler!
Even in Arabia, as I compute, Mahomet will have
exhausted himself, and become obsolete, while this
Shakspeare, this Dante, may still be young:—while this
Shakspeare may still pretend to be a priest of mankind,
of Arabia as of other places, for unlimited periods to
come! Compared with any speaker or singer one
knows, even with Æschylus or Homer, why should he
not, for veracity and universality, last like them? He
is *sincere* as they; reaches deep down, like them, to the
universal and perennial. But as for Mahomet, I think
it had been better for him *not* to be so conscious! Alas,
poor Mahomet! all that he was conscious of was a mere
error: a futility and triviality—as indeed such ever is.
The truly great in him, too, was the unconscious: that
he was a wild Arab lion of the desert, and did speak out
with that great thunder-voice of his, not by words which
he *thought* to be great, but by actions, by feelings, by a
history which *were* great! His Koran has become a
stupid piece of prolix absurdity; we do not believe, like
him, that God wrote that! The great man here, too,

as always is a force from the great deeps." So much for
Mahomet.

Napoleon almost shares the same fate; and in some
measure the praise of Burns is qualified. Napoleon, it
is admitted, held at first to fact, was zealous for order,
and knew no rest; but "an element of blameable ambi-
tion showed itself from the first in this man; gets the
victory over him at last, and involves him and his work
in ruin." In short, he became a liar and a quack in
giving himself over to the worship of outward force—
"whose conquests do not endure!" and so, in the long
run, he was thrown out and defeated, and went the way
all quacks are ultimately doomed to go. What was
heroic in him existed apart from that too, was far deeper
than that. He was not all a quack, but what was of the
quack in him greatly qualifies his greatness. "What
Napoleon did will, in the long run, amount to what he
did *justly;* what Nature with her laws will sanction. To
what of reality was in him; to that and nothing more.
The rest was all smoke and waste." In little things to
the end the heroic does peep through. In St. Helena it
is notable how he still insists on the practical, the real.
"Why talk and complain: above all, why quarrel with
one another?" he says to his poor discontented followers. There is no *result* in it; it comes to nothing
that one can *do.* Say nothing, if one can do nothing."
And so Napoleon, too, is dismissed with this almost
Rhadamanthine severity of judgment. And then, Car-

lyle's great love for Burns will not prevent his saying plainly that that hunt our bard held after some "rock of independence,"—some heaven in external circumstances, was false, self-conscious; and he turns away rather to the patient, pious old father, "swallowing down daily so many sore sufferings into silence;" thus approving himself more a hero by far than the speaking son. In this way does Carlyle set up and put down his own hero-types, not without purpose and significance; for he thereby only the more persistently points us to a pure and lofty principle of life, which may be carried into the' individual experience, and the fruit of which will be patient, valorous doing and enduring, without complaint or protest, or even so much as desire for any outward change. For truly "Here is our America, or nowhere." "Wealth richer than both the Indies lies everywhere for man, if he will endure."

In the essay on "Characteristics," to which reference has already been made, we have the distinction between the Conscious and the Unconscious wrought out with the utmost precision. Carlyle's works, to the very last volume of *Friedrich*, are but illustrations and illuminations of the principles there enunciated. "The Silent or the Unconscious is great—belongs to pure unmixed life; Consciousness, again, is little, a diseased mixture and conflict of life and death; Unconsciousness is the sign of creation; Consciousness, at best that of manufacture." And this principle is invariably applied in the judgment of human actions and human characters, and hence we have such utterances as these:—" The Shakspeare takes no airs for writing *Hamlet* and the *Tempest*, understands not that it is anything surprising; Milton, again, is more conscious of his faculty, which accordingly is quite an inferior one." . . . " Your hero is unconscious that he is a hero, that is a condition of all greatness." . . . " We reckon it a striking fact in Johnson's history, this unconsciousness and carelessness of his as to fame." . . . . " My friend, all speech and rumour is short-lived, foolish, untrue. Genuine work alone, what thou workest faithfully, that is eternal, as the Almighty Founder and World-builder himself. Stand, then, by that, and let ' Fame ' and the rest of it go prating." . . . . . And again, " Emerson is perhaps far less notable for what he has spoken or done than for the many things he has not spoken and has foreborne to do." This last little extract affords a deep glance into the whole principle on which Carlyle tests character and reads history. That a man should be asserted a hero or notable for forbearing to say and to do, and so making it wholly impossible for history to appropriate him in his highest hero-phase, is a puzzling enunciation. But in it nevertheless lies a truth, which has never for a moment ceased to be present to the mind of Carlyle, and might be rightly enough named his guiding truth. " Of the wrong we are always conscious, of the right never," is but another axiomatic way of expressing the same thing.

And so it not unnaturally comes about, that, of historical heroes, those are the greatest to Carlyle who have held assiduously by those common faculties of order, economy, and prudence, and who have by these been the means of securing great results for their brethren, their nation, and the world. The belief in the possession of special and peculiar gifts is but another form of the same false *consciousness* that made Mahomet believe he was specially " the Prophet of God." Such a belief, in its ultimate practical issue, comes to be sceptical, because it would necessarily lead the man who held it to regard himself as superior to the mass of men, and to live under the idea of a *conscious* separation and isolation from common ends and common interests. The end of all such feelings is, and can only be, misery. Nature makes no exceptions to her requirements; over all alike she suspends her Damocles' sword, if they obey her not faithfully. The genius who fancies his gifts will excuse his not doing his common duty like a common man must some day pay the smart in want of a dinner, or some such way. Chattertons chase shadows of fame, labouring at draw-wells whence comes no water; Hazlitts haunt London streets, hunger-stricken, because hit by an epigram and no longer able to work; Keatses actually court disease and death by lazily dreaming of Eldorados where certain finer appetites may be sated; and Coleridges, notwithstanding high gifts, are poor mendicants, at last dependent on the tendance and bounty of others.

I remember always, when thinking of such things, a remark I have seen somewhere about Schiller to the effect that he did all common things like a common man ; and recall too, as not without a significance in its way, Goethe's confession that " nothing had been sent to him in his sleep," and that he had had " a tough battle " always. Carlyle actually seems to delight in quoting these expressions of Goethe.

Paradoxical as it may appear, Carlyle's scheme of Heroes may thus properly be defined as the annihilation of the worship of genius in the commonly accepted sense of it. The men he most loves may possess high faculties, but that in itself is not the ground of his reverence for them. These faculties only become notable by a strong interfusion of the common, or at all events more universally attainable elements, of practical vigour, patience, courage, and tolerance. Out of the union of these springs reverence, which unites all the faculties under it as under a crown, giving unmistakeable " assurance of a *man.*" Carlyle's favourites are each great in the measure that they lived in that manly spirit, which it would be well for each of us to cultivate and live in. Samuel Johnson, Burns, Goethe, Friedrich the Great, are not perfect men by any means ; but they were all assiduous workers, held broadly by *sincerity*, hating all *cant* and sentimentality. Now, these may seem strong expressions ; more especially with regard to Freidrich, Carlyle's treatment of whom has to very many been a puzzle and a stumbling-block. It would not suit my purpose to go with any minuteness of detail into an analysis of Friedrich's History; I must, however, devote a word or two to it.

As a piece of literary work, these six volumes, it must be admitted, stand alone, alike for the pains-taking and veracious method pursued, the thoroughly original style, and for the many specimens of that wondrous word-painting which can only be properly designated by one epithet—Carlylean. But it is not alone as a literary effort in this sense that we have perused the latter portion especially with such pleasure, and so value the whole of it. The work is happily more than that. Properly taken, it is an illustration and application, from an extreme point of view it is true, but yet quite an allowable one, of the principles laid down by Carlyle ever since he began to write—the highest outcome of Carlyle's reflections upon man and life. In the first place it is intensely *realistic*, and that not only in manner, but in essence and spirit. The ideal, and all that pertains to it, is abnegated and cast down. Even the picture of the outward man of Friedrich is significant as a protest against carrying into history some notions of heroes apparently derived from classical poetry. Here we have no handsome Apollo six feet high, straight as a rush, and with everything grand and proper about him. Not at all. A rather round-shouldered, shambling drill-sergeant of a man, with nothing whatever of the soft or sentimental in his composition; pipe-clayed and commonplace, and with evident marks of haste and hard work upon him. There is only one captivating feature about the man, and that is the eye which really has some of the brightness and fire one would expect in an Achilles or a Hector. Otherwise Friedrich in his outer man is commonplace and unheroic utterly. The book throughout asserts and proves, too, that the greatest results flow from the careful prudent direction of common elements; and the lesson is, that each man in the measure that he acts manlike and truly governs himself, begins a good work,—lays the foundation, in fact, for all greatness, whether his duty lie in the way of governing men or not. Assuredly he will have some little kingdom to direct and guide, and sow influences in : order, economy, and prudent self-control will be of value there also, and will have good results. The same spirit carried into the little seedfield as Friedrich carried into his big one, will in the end be equally beneficial, though sometimes it may seem to the children that injustice is done in the distribution of the bread, and the neighbours complain about outlying bits of ground taken in, which they had allowed to run to waste or neglected to " take in."

Next, let it be said, that Friedrich wrought with a purpose. While Europe was sorrowfully falling under the hand of kings who ruled not, and the general structure of things was passing into that disorder whose legitimate fruit was revolution, Friedrich tried to be true to the place Providence had placed him in, and would not only pretend to rule but really do it. The king is said to be the servant of all; Friedrich would struggle to be so. He would do real kingly work in return for loyalty,—give guidance for service rendered. And not without some self-denial could Friedrich or any other man brace himself up to do so: work of this sort does not so readily commend itself to men's minds. Had he not his proclivities to write poetry and send verses and receive them? Had he not Voltaires and other elegant talkers who would have gladly made home at his court to pleasantly relieve his days; perhaps nights also? He liked ease naturally as the rest of us do. Ruling of men, incessant drilling and marching of them, was not so attractive as many other things Friedrich had tried, I can readily fancy! Yet he would not shirk his work; he would stay at his post. Poetry is very fine; but it is not all. If it is harmony indeed, how can a man come by it but by being first of all in harmony with himself and the things around him, and that, too, by wrestling with them and beating them first of all. So Friedrich must abandon his verse-writing, and give up Voltaires.

The next thing I would remark is that Friedrich was not a selfish man. Had he been so he would assuredly not have quite done as he did. He would not have given up the poetry which of course was vastly praised. He would most probably have stayed at home to study hexameters, and to joke pleasantly with literary buffoons! He would have done his drilling and fighting by deputy chiefly too, I think. But no. Friedrich is in this sense faithful, that if he declares war he will himself do a good share of the drilling, and also take his fair stroke of the fighting. There is something of honesty and genuine manhood in that one consideration. And then there *was* an unselfish element in all that fighting. It was all for the sake of his Prussia; that she might be great. Perhaps, too, a broader idea intermingled itself with the patriotic one,—that his conquests would be beneficial to the world by spreading Protestantism. That salutary element had entered deeply into the Prussian life, and distinguished the Prussian nation from the others. And though Friedrich never set up with methodistic self-examination to persuade himself as to the vast strength of his Protestantism, yet perhaps his Protestantism was all the stronger on that very account. At all events, without any loud boasting, he did Protestantism great service.

And let it be remarked at this point also, that there is a certain respect in which mights and rights are nearly alike—a sense, too, on which the Old Testament seems to look sometimes with at least a little favour. The Jews, when they had national and, as they conceived, good ends to serve, were not very particular about the rights of Canaanites on the whole. If Friedrich

5—2

of Prussia wronged great powers, these powers were themselves based on wrong and lived by it, and their titles to vast stretches of territory it would not have been easy to show. Their right to them had gone when they were so weak, Romanized and divided as not to be able to keep them ; and if Austria was not so then, she was on the way to it. But this may also be asserted, that had Friedrich seized some of the Papal principalities of Germany besides poor, openly Prussian, Jesuit-ridden, more-than-three-fourths Protestant Silesia, he would have done vast good. A great share of the political difficulties of Europe have sprung out of the peculiar position in which the Protestant and Romish states stand to each other, and the constant jealousies shown toward the Protestants by the Catholics. A fight has yet to be fought with regard to ascendancy between these two, which Friedrich saw and was prepared to take his part in when he so decisively asserted a Protestant faith, quietly putting down Jesuits and "other extraneous persons." That too was something which Protestants might admire, if they would only try to look for themselves.

As to Friedrich's sincerity or insincerity I may say that it is one thing to be false in words and another to be false to facts. Many men are very correct, never "tell a lie," and yet whose lives are simply one great falsehood. The man in the parable, who at first refused and afterwards went to the vineyard, was commended; but the one who promised and went not, was condemned. The parable may have its vital application to our time also!

Carlyle, with that pious honesty which characterizes him, at the very outset of the work indicates the somewhat low ground on which he receives Friedrich as a hero. He is not blind to Friedrich's faults, nay, can canvass them perhaps as well as any one: but he finds that the centre of the man, whence sprung his activities, his greatnesses, lay quite apart from these. And Carlyle is quite consistent in this respect, too, that Friedrich is an *unconscious* sort of hero, scarcely knowing how great and valiant and brave he is:—

"Friedrich is by no means one of the perfect demigods; and there are various things to be said against him with good ground. To the last a questionable hero; with much in him that one could have wished not there, and much wanting which one could have wished. But there is one feature which strikes you at an early period of the inquiry. That in his way he is a reality—that he always means what he speaks; grounds his actions, too, on what he recognizes for the truth; and, in short, has nothing whatever of the hypocrite or phantasm. . . . For he knew well, to a quite uncommon degree, and with a *merit all the higher that it was an unconscious one,* how entirely inexorable is the nature of facts, whether recognized or not, ascertained or not; how vain all cunning of diplomacy, management, and sophistry to save any mortal who does *not* stand on the truth of things, from sinking in the long run." The relation the work holds to history generally is that of a protest against the habit of importing something quite imaginary to help out the idea of a hero; and it contains also a constant assertion of the fact, that in the real, rightly discerned, the ideal or truly heroic will be found to lie waiting for disimprisonment, like that damsel we read of in knightly chronicles, who, rudely bound to a tree, had to wait for her appointed deliverer. The real seen truly in its relations not only to the time but to all the past and all the future, is alone the genuine ideal.*

Carlyle's *Friedrich* and Goethe's *Wilhelm Meister* are one in spirit and purpose. The idea of both alike is to show by living examples that mere loftiness of gift or endowment is nothing; that it is the spirit which transfigures life; that the consecration of common gifts to high and unselfish ends ought to be the real aim of all; and that this, indeed, is the only way to lasting greatness. Both rightly read proclaim the rich possibilities that lie in man's nature to be and to do. Carlyle seems to say: "Here is Friedrich now, by no means a genius as you reckon genius, and yet see what he can make of life simply by being industrious, orderly, economic, true." Goethe, again, whispers to us mildly and wisely—"This young Meister is a sort of milksop,

---

* The reader is referred to Addenda, "Friedrich Wilhelm," p. 247.

wasting his youthful days in self-indulgence, or at best theatrical dilettantism, yet behold what he can attain by simply following with a great purpose the idea of duty and the infinite significance of life to which he has at length clearly awakened. His very simplicity and open inquiring honesty of mind keep him from growing conceited, yet sometimes seem to hinder his progress; but ultimately and really all things serve him, because he has got to live in a right and earnest spirit." And, indeed, may it not be said that the glory of our friend Abbot Samson in *Past and Present*, is that he, too, justifiably thrusts himself forward, modestly yet firmly, into view here? Samson put away from him all prurient ambitions about literature and empty dreams of fame, answered to the call of Providence, set about doing real work, and by assiduous application, insight, decision, and economy, he, too, brought about order, peace, and fruitfulness in his distracted world of the Abbey of St. Edmunds.

I have seen statements to the effect that Carlyle's worship of intellect, of genius, or of force, had bred in him a contempt for humanity generally—a scorn for the ordinary run of men, and for those common lowly interests of life, which for the " dim moiling millions " must ever be the chief concern. A more short-sighted and unjust remark it would indeed be difficult to make. As I have shown, mere intellect or lofty endowment of any sort is not with Carlyle the prime matter. The great question with him is rather how these have been used, and to what results they have led—how this man or that man has applied, first of all, these faculties he held in common with his fellows; in one word, in what *spirit* he has wrought, whether with great faculties or with little. For, according to Carlyle, every faculty of man has open for it two possible channels of expression —the sphere of silent duty in the fulfilment of the ordinary social relations; and the loud, noisy, self-conscious proclamation of itself through literature or art. Every true or approximately true expression through the latter medium must arise either from a beautiful harmonious living and doing, or from an intensely clear perception of the beauty of these in the lives of others. Literature, in all the phases of it—poetry, fiction, biography, history—is but a selection and presentment of the heroic as the writer viewed it and felt it. He can write to no purpose till he has been captivated and made to admire; he will not write grandly till he has even loved and worshipped.

For complete sympathy is the bond which reunites literature to life. Sympathy—going out of self—is the mystic channel by which in fact streams of health are poured into the one from the other. Thus, therefore, speaks Carlyle, in the third of the lectures on Heroes,—

" Find a man whose words paint you a likeness, you have found a man worth something; mark his manner of doing it as very characteristic of him. In the first place he could not have discerned the object at all, or seen the type of it, unless he had, what we may call, *sympathised* with it—had in him sympathy to bestow on objects. He must have been sincere about it, too; sincere and sympathetic; a man without worth cannot give you the likeness of any object; he dwells in vague outwardness, fallacy, and hearsay about all objects. And indeed may we not say that intellect altogether expresses itself in discerning what an object is? . . . . And how much of *morality* is in the kind of insight we get of anything; 'the eye seeing in all things what it brought with it, the faculty of seeing.' To the mean eye all things are trivial, as certainly as to the jaundiced eye they are all yellow."

Of course Carlyle knows as well as any one that the loftiest of our literary men have been good haters too. But then, genuine hate is only an inverse form of love. " It was not out of hatred to the opponent, but love to the thing opposed," says Carlyle, " that Johnson became cruel, fiercely contradictory; it was only when his religion, the Church of England, or the Divine Right were impugned that he burst out. These were his symbols of all that was good and precious for men; his very ark of the covenant; whoso touched them rudely tore asunder his very heart of hearts."

But after all the highest claims of literature must yield to the sterner calls of work and duty. And so again Carlyle says of Abbot Samson,—"Three pound ten, and a life of literature, especially of quiet literature, without copyright, or world-celebrity of literary gazettes, —yes, thou brave Abbot Samson, for thyself it had been better, easier, perhaps also nobler! But then for thy disobedient monks, unjust viscounts; for a domain of St. Edmund overgrown with solecisms, human or other, it had not been so well. Nay, neither could *thy* literature, never so quiet, have been easy. Literature, when noble, is not easy; but only when ignoble. Literature, too, is a quarrel and internecine duel with the whole world of darkness that lies without one and within one; rather a hard fight at times even with the three pound ten secure. Thou, there where thou art, wrestle and duel along cheerfully to the end, and make no remarks."

Every true book is a new assertion of the higher in man, and a showing how, if the man is true to himself, this will develop itself even through the most unpromising of forms or circumstances. *Wilhelm Meister*, in this point of view, is, as has already been said, one of the most peculiar books, and the hero a very perplexing one. The man who would read *Wilhelm Meister* merely as a story, and without reference to the healthful flower of life which grows out of simple openness and honesty of mind, realizing itself fully at length in the enjoyment of all that was pure, elevating, kindly, and noble— would read the book to no good purpose, because he would not have the least sympathy with the spirit out of which it was written. Wilhelm Meister was no genius, in that respect, he was truly no hero; but he awakened to high aims; the idea rose upon him with the utmost clearness, that man exists for something more than to eat, sleep, dream, and enjoy himself; and the spirit in which he acted upon the idea, and the measure in which he realized his aspirations, raise him to the heroic. His want of special gifts keeps him in union with the common run of men; the *spirit* in which he casts down his low desires and tendencies, and mounts to the clear region of wisdom, unites him with the serene lofty brotherhood of heroes. Thus Carlyle finds it compatible with his severe, yet kindly philosophy, so to admire the book. For it is a preaching forth of human possibilities; but in the broadest sense. Every man may attain what Wilhelm Meister attained, by simply working in the spirit in which at length he resolved to work. There is a consecration in *Wilhelm Meister* after which there is no longer any of that hard, economic or prosaic limitation which at first repelled Novalis. It melts into poetry. As spring subdues the hard, heavy, rigorous influences of winter (in which each individual force seems to sit isolated), and softens all into a fluent harmony of movement, so does the light of a new purpose in *Wilhelm Meister*. The glory of the book is that it is commonplace, and that the common is at length so transfigured by high and noble aims as to become truly romantic.

As Carlyle admires Wilhelm Meister, so he cherishes

many characters that history has been inclined to
scoff at. He has drawn poor Bozzy from the well in
which his too conceited brother critics and biographers
had cast him, on account (according to themselves) of
the very sin of which they were yet more guilty than he
was. Boswell, says Carlyle, *was* a sort of zany, but he
was wise in clinging, through all contempt and scorn, to
the wisest man of his time, though he found him in
rags and steeped in poverty ; and because poor Bozzy
wrought in a right spirit, although so wanting in faculty,
he has produced the best biography of modern times,
and has taken his place among the great. In life and in
literature Carlyle estimates not by gifts but by the *spirit*
in which real work has been done. Hence in both alike
he is inclined to condemn much that seems great and is
commonly received as such,—to kick down the idols, like
a true iconoclast, and with a sardonic grin of satisfaction
to contemplate the rattling wreck and ruin ; and then,
perhaps, with darkened brow, he turns away into the
obscurest corner, and snatches out of the dust and darkness some unknown or scarce known name, and surrounds
it with a halo of light. The silent fulfilment of duty in
any sphere he so admires and loves. The size of the
seedfield is nothing, the cultivation of it is the all in all.
And as this idea has not been a common one among
historians and literary men, it is not by any means
surprising that Carlyle should have often to protest, both
with respect to what literature has preserved and what

it has forgotten. He is sometimes inclined to figure history as a sort of sieve, which allows the seed to run through, and holds only that which is valueless. And the reason is that historians have only dealt with the external-great; and forgotten that the soul of any given period was the unknown, or but half-known select few reverent, devout souls. In *Sartor Resartus* we are told that George Fox's making to himself a suit of leather is the one incident in modern history, though silently passed over by most historians. It was so for this reason—that in a period of artificiality and division, the assertion of religious independence and manly individuality was the very form which the new truth at that moment most needed to take.

But how uniformly tender our teacher is to the poor, the unfortunate! What a heart for those who are weary and heavy-laden, halting and stumbling under the load of life. The poor mother of Jean Paul, so good but querulous, misses not her meed of praise, for she has fought her sore fight of life with a valiant womanly heart, though now she so fears, and faints, and falters; the mother of squalid, filthy Marat, too, passes in a moment before our eyes, and Marat is once again a child, lovely, serene, and pure upon her breast; even the poor outcast to whom Samuel Johnson said, "No, no, my girl, it won't do," lives mildly in our imagination, because Carlyle has touched her with the halo of his human love. A softer, more tender, generously-responsive

heart hardly beats in London to-day than Carlyle's.   Let
a man with even half a heart read these words, and then
say if Carlyle could be scornful or contemptuous of the
lowly or the unfortunate :—

" That unhappy outcast, with all her sins and woes,
her lawless desires, too complex mischances, her wailings
and her riotings, has departed utterly ; alas ! her siren
finery has got all besmutched, ground, generations since,
into dust and smoke ; of her degraded body and whole
miserable earthly existence, all is away : *she* is no longer
here, but far from us in the bosom of eternity—whence
we, too, came, whither we, too, are bound ! Johnson said,
' No, no, my girl ; it won't do ;' and herewith the
wretched one, seen but for the twinkling of an eye,
passes on into the utter darkness.   No high Calista that
ever issued from storyteller's brain, will impress us more
deeply than this meanest of the mean ; and for a good
reason—that *she* issued from the Maker of men."

With regard to the poor day-worker, Carlyle is constantly disburthening himself of the most touching and
pitiful passages.   Passing by the now so celebrated one
in *Sartor Resartus,* beginning—" Two Men I honour
and no third "—this other may be extracted from *Past
and Present :*—" Pity him, too, the Hard-handed, with
bony brow, rudely combed hair, eyes looking out as in
labour, in difficulty and uncertainty : rude mouth, the
lips coarse, loose, as in hard toil and lifelong fatigue
they have got the habit of hanging :—hast thou seen

aught more touching than the rude intelligence, so cramped yet energetic, unsubduable, true, which looks out of that marred visage ? Alas, and his poor wife, with her own hands, washed that cotton neckcloth for him, buttoned that coarse shirt, sent him forth creditably trimmed as she could. In such imprisonment lives he for his part : man cannot now deliver him : the red pulpy infant has been baked and fashioned *so*.

" Or what kind of baking was it that the other mortal got which has baked him into the genus Dandy ? Elegant Vacuum : serenely looking upon all Plenums and Entities as low and poor to his serene Chimership and *Non*-entity laboriously attained ! Heroic Vacuum ; inexpugnable, while purse and present condition of society hold out ; curable by no hellebore. The doom of Fate was—Be thou a Dandy ! Have thy eye-glasses, opera glasses, thy Long Acre cabs with white-breeched tiger, thy yawning impassivities, pococurantisms ; *fix* thyself in dandyhood, undeliverable ; it is thy doom."

A more tremblingly affectionate heart for all that has the ring of real about it does not beat. He would willingly give his right hand to procure guidance of the best for the millions baked into imprisonment of labour : his great complaint was and is that they are not guided but *left alone*. As another specimen of the glow and glory with which he ever seeks to surround true hand-labour take this :—

" Manchester, with its cotton fuz, its smoke and dust,

its tumult and contentious squalor, is hideous to thee? Think not so : a precious substance, beautiful as magic dreams, and yet no dream but a reality, lies hidden in that noisome wrappage ;—a wrappage struggling indeed (look at chartism and such like) to cast itself off, and leave the beauty free and visible there! Hast thou heard, with sound ears, the awakening of a Manchester, on Monday morning, at half-past five by the clock; the rushing off of its thousand mills, like the boom of an Atlantic tide, ten thousand times ten thousand spools and spindles all set humming there,—it is perhaps, if thou knew it well, sublime as a Niagara, or more so. Cotton-spinning is the clothing of the naked in its result ; the triumph of man over matter in its means. Soot and despair are not the essence of it; they are divisible from it,—at the hour, are they not crying fiercely to be divided? The great Goethe, looking at cotton Switzerland, declared it, I am told, to be of all things that he had seen in the world the most poetical. Whereat friend Kanzler Von Müller, in search of the palpable picturesque, could not but stare wide-eyed. Nevertheless, our World-poet knew well what he was saying !"

Napoleon's book on Julius Cæsar has called forth a good deal of clever and some very hornheaded criticism, into which Carlyle's name has been most unwarrantably dragged. Carlyle is once more declared a believer in Destiny—a Fatalist, and so forth, simply because he has given the name of Hero-worship to some lectures.

Names are strange things, and may convey very different meanings to persons of different culture; but the man who would associate Napoleon the Third and Thomas Carlyle together as Hero-worshippers, has certainly very little power to detect a meaning the least recondite, and as little insight into character. The schemes of the two men are properly the very antipodes of each other. They start from different and opposing points, and also reach different results. Napoleon departs from the deliverances of history as to the benefit conferred on nations by the advent of men of a certain type of mind and character, whose failure in any respect is declared to be a national misfortune and a loss to the world, and whose death by force is, and has always been, equivalent to national suicide. The very idea of a man in an obvious, but yet half-secret way, instituting a comparison of the outer incidents of the lives of two heroes and the circumstances they lived among for the purpose of justifying and interpreting the one by the other, proves clearly enough the truth of this assertion about Napoleon's point of departure. But Carlyle, on the other hand, starts from the idea of faith properly. The unseen and vital contact with it, or in other words harmony with the divine law, is most distinctly announced as the ground of heroism; the hero's true triumphs are declared to lie in the will, which can free itself wholly from all power of " Circumstance," or Fate, or Destiny, however named—using and embracing these elements even while it despises them ; Napoleon's system, in fact, is the worship of an almost Pagan Naturalism and an iron self-consciousness ; Carlyle's is the complete annihilation of both these ; the one believes in destiny, and scouts the idea of Providence ; the other declares men's freedom, re-establishes Providence, and sees the one united with the other in all the phenomena of life ; the one would say that Napoleon the Great succeeded so far, and was destined to defeat at a certain point because such and such circumstances existed in combination at the time ; the other would say he was unsuccessful because he was not true enough, wise enough, just enough, or in other words, deflected too far from the law of God. The Emperor claims a certain arbitrary right for Cæsar, Napoleon, and such men over others who should render a blind, fateful obedience ; Carlyle declares the power of such men over their fellows only to be real and lasting in itself, or good in its influences, precisely as it is in harmony with those laws to which men are constantly called by Heaven itself to be loyal and to obey, and that only in that measure are men bound to obey or are blessed in their obedience ; Napoleon is sceptical, material, saying that if circumstances had been other results had been different ; Carlyle says that everything prospers only as it is of God, or in other words, in the measure it has good and truth bound up in it, and that true victory is often gained through apparent or outward defeats. In short, as the points of departure were different, so the results are; circumstances with the one are supreme, "circumstance" with the other is put under by self-denial and noble unconsciousness of all power—or rights or claims over others. The one scheme is Pagan from first to last, the other is truly Christian; in these few words the whole difference is summed up.

Carlyle has high experiences which may not be written of, save as concerns their more practical results. He will not sentimentalize. "Do you want a man *not* to practise what he believes, then keep him often speaking of it in words," he says in effect repeatedly. And so he justifies his reticence with regard to those more purely spiritual matters,—the Future, and several others. They belong to the sphere of the "unspeakable," he constantly reminds us. "The Chief or the Three" in *Wilhelm Meister*, after having explained to the hero the significance of that strangely-arranged and strangely-suggestive picture gallery, brings him back at last to the door they started from, significantly leaving one chamber, and that the inmost one, unexplained and unexplored. The Chief makes a promise that next year, when Wilhelm returns, he may be admitted into the "Sanctuary of Sorrow." But strangely enough Goethe is reticent. He never conducts us along with his hero there. So Carlyle. He furnishes each one, so to speak, with practical outfit, which if acted upon will assuredly conduct to that victorious life-assurance in which all these things are opened, but only thereby become the more sacred and unspeakable. Towards *Him,*—"the greatest of all heroes," Carlyle cherishes burning, boundless reverence. Refers to Him, perhaps, eight or nine times in the course of his writings, but never even names Him; " Him we name not here;" " That sacred of names we name not here," are the phrases he uses, which surely, in a time of loud talking and light use of words once sacred may be regarded as the outcome of the deepest of all reverence. Many passages from Carlyle's books, more especially the *Latter-day Pamphlets,* might be quoted to show how thoroughly this man has vanquished doubt, and builds and settles himself upon belief.

As to Art, it can readily enough be imagined from what has been already written, that in this sphere he is "dreadful to purify," like Agamemnon's son. Art in all the phases of it has got to rest on a false basis. It has divorced itself from Reality—Truth; is no longer moral, and has consequently come to be no more guided by genuine insight. The true in heart alone can see clearly. Vision is conditioned by goodness—the foundation of art and literature as well, is pious sympathy with the good that is embodied or bound up in all human things, and is constantly struggling towards freer developments. The ideal dwells ever in the real. Romance reposes on every-day life as a statue on its pedestal; springs out of it indeed, and is for ever inseparable from it. The artist, therefore, should interpret the confused appearances, and show forth the victorious nature of good as against all partial, insincere, incomplete renderings, which often tend to teach that the good may be vanquished, which it never can by any possibility be. Art has become a thing of dress and circumstance; fantastic fripperiness of style and trick of finish are its main objects; the ideal truly has gone out, and empty fancy has come in, and that because artists have forsaken the field of fact. The loftiest pieces of art-criticism of this century are to be found in the two pamphlets—*Jesuitism* and *Hudson's Statue*, in which any inquiring artistic mind will find ample material for a few weeks' quiet reflection—say, during a sketching trip in Wales, or Italy, or the Scottish Highlands.

I had a good deal more to say of Carlyle's position with regard to creeds, and also something about his peculiar style, which for the present must remain unsaid. Perhaps as well—first, because those in such a position as I have taken up should not be careful to justify on little points a man whose long life-work has been to restore vital belief in goodness, and to make reverence once more the guiding influence of men's lives; and, secondly, because a man who really has got thoughts and truths to impart to us, and not the merest shadows of thoughts and truths, should be allowed to do it in his own way. The benefit is all on our side, and as we would never find fault with the mere order of a hospitable entertainment to which we had been invited, so should we not here. To get at the essential meaning is the one thing for us.

And so with a heart full of gratitude for great benefits received; for light which has helped to a surer tread through life; for a more vital faith in truth and goodness than was felt before; and for a deeper reverence which has made the universe more significant and beautiful and divine—I take leave of Thomas Carlyle; only hoping that these pages may not fail entirely of one object—to lead others earnestly and with open minds to commune with him as I have done in the spare moments of a busy life.

ALFRED TENNYSON,

THE MAN AND THE POET.

It has hitherto been the practice when writing of poets, accredited or unaccredited, to begin with subtle and often high-sounding disquisitions on the theory of poetry, or to attempt new definitions of it. Neither of these things do I aspire at accomplishing in this essay. Such tasks will best be left to other hands. Poetry is like life in this, that it eludes all attempts to close and fix it in definitions, and will not square itself off with theories, any more than the sea will remain at one level. Your critics perfect quite a little system of their own, and unitedly declare that no one shall be henceforth admitted into the poetic guild who does not strictly submit to it. A Burns or a Wordsworth comes along, and with one breath puffs the critical cobweb away; and, rising sheer above all such trammels, pours forth so clearly and truthfully his simple subtle music, that later students can only smile at the already almost forgotten critics who proscribed him.

Science, by the aid of a prism, can so far decompose a sunbeam. It can, by analysis, reveal to us some truths which, however, only point us further forward into mystery; at last science itself sinks back baffled even here; and to speak of its ever analysing the sun "that floods the world with light" is altogether out of the question. Nor can criticism ever wholly comprehend poetry in itself, or exhaust it in abstract canons. It must humbly follow rather, as the moon the sun. The very light that the critic reads by, the poet has brought to him; and how can he analyse or define successfully the very medium of his seeing? From the poet primarily all rules of criticism are derived, and only in each great poet is to be found the true standard by which he is to be judged. Genuine criticism directed towards one worthy the name of an acknowledged singer thus becomes a far harder task than is usually supposed. The critic must study the man through his works, and become *acquainted* with him before he has the warrant to write a sentence. It is easy to detect faults of form; not so easy to direct the minds of others into tracks of inward meaning, which can only be discerned as the inner meanings of nature, as expressed in her minuter forms and changes, are discerned, by intense, patient observation and even communion.

Though much criticism has already been directed towards Tennyson, his secret—or in other words the new revelation of truth he has brought us—has not yet been wholly exhausted. The truth is, Tennyson has been hitherto treated rather too exclusively from a formal standpoint, dealt with as an artist as that word has in recent years come to be understood, and almost indiscriminately applied to fluent versifiers and arrant pretentious bunglers of all sorts. Our business with Tennyson is to be of a closer, more vital character. We shall attempt to decipher the man from his works, to show how far and how faithfully he has mirrored himself, though indirectly, in these published poems of his, and how much the poet in this case, as in all cases, owes to the man. An important task truly, but one whose difficulty is in a ratio with its importance, as indeed always happens! Were even a respectable measure of success attained, however, the result would doubtless be welcomed by the many who are now interested in all that is said regarding him, and also by the few who are unsettled, and searching eagerly for truth, honestly inquiring what the great poet or rhythmic teacher of the age really means, and what his chief aims and ends are. Whether the following pages justify me in saying that I have given a fresh and worthy view of Alfred Tennyson as one of our great teachers, is a matter that remains with my readers to decide. The attempt has been honestly made, not without glances back at the sad mistakes of Jeffreys, Giffords, and their followers, who still figure to their own profit in newspapers and magazines, treating poetry as a thing of musical lines and single shining metaphors, and shutting out the fact that poetry is a grandly vital spiritual thing like nature itself.

Readers are therefore not troubled with the usual paragraphs of stereotyped analyses. My notion is and has long been that the one thing for a critic is to discover what a man who comes before him as a true poet really means, to detect his inward harmonies of being from which must spring his outer music, to see and to show his deeper purpose—how on the one hand he has been baffled, has fallen, sinned, doubted, been pained, crossed, and disappointed; and on the other how he has borne that, the joys that have visited him, the victories he has shared—in one word, how he has fought, aspired, and through it all reached that inward harmony of life which alone could enable him to sing greatly and to purpose.

This notion of poetry it will readily be seen is one which leads us to study more the inward spirit than the outer form—more the soul and life out of which the verse has sprung than the verse itself. For, as I believe that everything a man does or can do partakes of the very essence of his character, and will discover it to those who have insight enough, so the man may be held to lie within the poet hidden from the casual eye, it may be, as the roots of the beautiful full-flowered acacia are hidden, but not the less really the very source of poetic life. It shall be by illustrations rather than by dogmatic argument I shall try to establish this principle— that personal character is the test and ultimate measure of poetry, and that true poetry can only spring from lofty life. It may, however, be simply remarked here, that as no material body can transgress gravitation, so no poet can really rise above his own life or experience. Men may put in words a great many traditional things, and give utterance very beautifully to long-transmitted truths; but if these have not passed through the very furnace of heart and brain, they will not be struck out with that directness and beautiful simplicity which can anew stamp them with vitality, and give them a right to live and be loved by men. Byron's poems, from beginning to end, suggest an aspiring, discontented, highly-gifted but inwardly divided man, who has never reached in himself that peacefully harmonious fulness which alone can give the highest tone to poetry—the consecration and reconcilement one might name it. Keats again exhausted his life in a sort of spiritualized sensations, and one reads it in every line he wrote. His ideal of life, indeed, seems to have been to have got lain on a downy sofa to lazily muse, and forgetting all common every-day things and duties, to dream wonderful dreams and record them with golden pen, angels meanwhile fanning him with their wings. Thus all his compositions alike suggest a dreamy, indolently-luxurious half-sensuous repose, and in reading them one cannot help being for the time touched by it. Hence, to the active practical mind Keats can never recommend himself. And as the world requires workers—men and women to live " a battle and a march " life from day to day—Keats can never be a broadly-popular poet.   He wants sinew, and must actually have wanted it corporeally, and was therefore but an incomplete man, and an incomplete singer. Samuel Taylor Coleridge's " Hymn Written at Sunrise in the Vale of Chamouni," is a very beautiful poem ; it has a stately ring about it, and the march of the music is Miltonic.   But even here the character of the man peeps through ; for nature actually seems to. overpower the individual will, and to prostrate it ; and thus Coleridge's life defect,—want of will, a helpless, almost passive submission before beautiful or majestic material forms, marks and mars his finest poem, and runs in, disturbing that lofty spirit, even as it becomes religious, and struggles to worship.

To justify criticism—in any sense deeper than captious formal fault-finding—there must, then, in this way of thinking, be insight and thorough sympathy. Criticism thus becomes essentially a study of noble, struggling human lives ; for little true poetry was ever written that was not doubly fought for : first in a battle in which the poet is but a representative of humanity, and next in a struggle to embody that in suitable form which is peculiar to him as poet.   The poet, in a word, studies life in himself and others, and by the intensity of his experience is urged to write ; but the energy and heavy breathing occasioned by the effort are apt to dim the word-pictures he produces.   The critic, too, studies life, not, however, with the direct aim of reconstructing, but rather that he may be enabled faithfully to remove any dimness that merely, from the special circumstances of the poet, may have attached to the outer form into which he has run his thought, his experience. It is in this spirit, and remembering the sanctities of poetry as well as the responsibilities of reviewing, that Alfred Tennyson is now humbly and lovingly approached.

Tennyson is possessed of rare gifts, and, with a care and zeal seldom witnessed, these have been cultivated from his earliest years. His course, indeed, has been one of constant progress and elevation. During the period when crowds of other young poets foolishly overflow with surges of passion "perplexing nations," Tennyson studiously set about perfecting his instruments, and strictly eschewed dealing with real life and incident till he had reached mature manhood. His first efforts—Mermen, Mermaids, his Sea-Fairies, his Adelines, his Marianas, and his Isabels—are mere imaginative lay-figures set up for the poet to work upon; and no one knows better, or feels more deeply, the want of real soul in these than, I am persuaded, does the laureate himself. For although we have all the outer perfection of form in these, they are, to use a paradox, perhaps just a little too perfect, lucid, and self-contained to be of the highest poetry.

The self-command indicated in this judicious slowness to meddle with real life is a notable phenomenon in Tennyson's life, and might with profit be pointed out to those who talk about his "sensitive unrest and fevered impetuosity." His characteristic as a man is intensity; his characteristic as an artist is repose, rounded completeness; that, however, being sometimes seen in his subtle suggestions more than in defined form. When he came to deal with real life, he soon found that his complete command over words—a power so valuable in itself and indispensable to the poet—would yet only in this sphere carry him a certain way, and because, as Goethe has said, "the deepest cannot be expressed in words," he in practice soon departed from the Goethean example, and never sought to paint separate isolated moods or phases of passion. That stops the moment he begins to deal with the real. "The May Queen" and "The Miller's Daughter" are true pictures of English character and customs, and might be quoted as genuine poetic photographs, only they give what no photograph ever yet gave—that subdued richness of colouring which springs from an intensely-emotional nature duly controlled. The poet, we see, is now more and more subordinating the emotional in his experience, and on that very account his pictures are the more suggestive because his keen feeling, instead of obtrusively forcing itself into special and morbid utterances, subtly plays forth and mixes itself with the subject he treats. With all these pictures, such as the "Gardener's Daughter" and "Dora," the very deepest thoughts and rules of life are interwoven. In the latter, for instance, we see the triumph of affection over blind self-will, and the consequent beautiful reconciliation. Then, as if the poet felt a call to battle with the real problems of the day, he begins to weep a little over giant sins and destructive conventionalities. But he soon discovers that the tearful mood is a most unprofitable one, and so, to relieve his sorrow, he turns back with dim eyes to the dead past for a form through which to reflect the present—its virtues, its vices. In the earnest toying he holds, whether with old Greek forms or the world of Arthurian legend, we discover he has but one purpose, and that is to speak to the age. On this account, Tennyson was the true laureate long before he got that laurel—

> Greener from the brows
> Of him that uttered nothing base.

A doubt might, perhaps, reasonably be expressed as to whether he does not sometimes still shrink from *directly* facing the problems of the time; but, if so, this only shows the more what a mixture of prudence there is in his nature since his later poems have so abundantly proved his fitness as a poet to grapple with such themes. He loves to deal with old ideas and old garments of thought. But before he will use these they must each have yielded up to him a pure human gem—he must have found embodied in them broad human truths, which, anew, he sets to music showing their relation to our time, the lesson they have for ourselves.

√　　Perhaps the best illustration of his power and skill
in this respect is in that fine poem about Ulysses—the
much-suffering, far-travelled man, who was tossed away
on Calypso's isle when returning from the war of Troy,
and who, when, after another ten years, he did get
home, could not rest there, but with some of his
companions was fabled to have set out to seek the
Happy Isles, where dwells "the great Achilles whom
we knew." Tennyson's Ulysses is properly a luminous
forecast of his greater attempts at solving the problem of
Fate and Will; and here we have it represented faithfully from the highest old Greek point of view, if, indeed,
we have not, in the articulated musings of the ancient
hero, the old heathen idea, as it were, beautifully transfigured by a dim Christian hope. Thus he closes his
musings :—

> Though much is taken, much abides, and tho'
> We are not now that strength which in old days
> Moved earth and heaven, that which we are, we are,
> One equal temper of heroic hearts—
> Made weak by time and fate, but strong in will
> To strive, to seek, to find, and not to yield.

And what constitutes the essential grandeur at once
of these old Greek and later half-Christian or Arthurian
renderings of Tennyson is, that greatness is so directly
associated with moral purity. Sir Galahad has "a virgin
heart in work and will;" and so Tennyson, seizing the
higher fact, finds music consonant with it, and brings
back to us the whole soul of the old chivalry, which had

become degraded and obscured by the forms in which it had been preserved through hundreds of years. Mark the deep Christian truth of this verse :—

> My good blade carves the casques of men,
> My tough lance thrusteth sure,
> My strength is as the strength of ten,
> *Because my heart is pure.*

The *Morte d'Arthur*, too, is richly significant; yet not so much perhaps for itself—though some of the finest metaphors and most finished blank-verse lines in the language are to be found in it—as for the way in which the poet informs us of its relation to our time and all time. The poem gets a fine touch of modern life by an introduction and ending, possibly written long after the body of the poem itself, and there, especially in the ending, the broad human meaning of the legend is for the first time clearly wrought out, giving us the valuable key-note to all Tennyson's later Arthurian and classical poems. Thus these legendary poems, which form such a large section of Tennyson's volumes, though much admired for their exquisite form and rounded finish, yet derive their real value from the broad hold they have of human nature and human instincts; and they are directly related to our time by some cunning amalgam or spiritual affinity of which Tennyson is more master than any other English poet, Spenser even not excepted : for Spenser often lost hold upon it in the search after an exact and exhaustive inner symbolism,

7

so that his poem has an arbitrary aspect such as we never meet with in those of the laureate. The close of the "Death of King Arthur," is most valuable as definitively pointing out his broad and vital system of interpretation, which fully justifies the deepest meanings being drawn from his later classical poems such even as at first sight might seem forced and capricious. Indeed, were it not that his poems are uniformly so staid and serious in spirit, it might be difficult to have the real interpretation in any sense received. The following lines are nobly expressive in the sense I have now been indicating :—

> In sleep, I seemed
> To sail with Arthur under looming shores,
> Point after point ; till on to dawn, when dreams
> Begin to feel the truth and stir of day,
> To me, methought, who waited with a crowd,
> There came a bark that, blowing forward, bore .
> King Arthur, like a modern gentleman
> Of stateliest port ; and all the people cried,
> " Arthur is come again ; he cannot die."
> Then those that stood upon the hills behind
> Repeated,—" Come again, and thrice as fair ; "
> And, further inland, voices echoed—" come,
> With all good things, and war shall be no more."
> At this a hundred bells began to peal,
> That, with the sound, I woke, and heard indeed
> The clear church-bells ring in the Christmas morn.

This is just Tennyson's way of saying that Arthur is the symbol of perfect *gentlemanhood;* and that so long as characters are refined by Christian influences, and go softly through the commonest duties of life, dispensing blessing and comfort, Arthur will be with us "thrice as fair;" and that if all men were embued with this spirit wars would cease upon the earth.

Of *In Memoriam* I would fain speak a little more fully. The main reason for introducing it at this point will afterwards appear. The preface to it beginning, "Strong Son of God, Immortal Love," may be regarded as the centre-point of the poet's life-plan or scheme of the universe. Just as Dante's whole works have their root in a sonnet or two in the *Vita Nuova*, so these wonderful verses point to the tap-root experience of our poet, whence has sprung his ripened greatness. But that does not lie in the fact of his having been bereaved —of his having "loved and lost;" and his commemorating his loss in a lengthened poem. In never-to-be-forgotten words he rejects the comfort proffered in the fact of loss being common to the race, and indirectly hints at that which was to distinguish his from a common sorrow. This lay in the wealth of being it was to bring him, which could never be fully said or sung, but only lived and rejoiced in. It is because he conquered sorrow, and made it yield him, and that not for himself alone, such a harvest of higher life and nobler aims, that he would have been, though he had never written a line—a poet. Like Dante, Tennyson draws great spiritual gain from his personal loss, and his sorrow becomes a platform from which to reach forward to loftier levels of life. Dante's poem is infinitely more valuable to us for showing so clearly, albeit by symbols, his gradual but glorious ascent upward through such hard harsh opposing circumstances, than for all its old-world philosophy and middle-age learning. Tennyson's *In Memoriam* is great for the same reason. It will live, not because the poet " advanced into the rare sphere of metaphysics ; " but because in it we clearly see philosophy transfigured by earnestness of life and aspirations after purity and holiness. From the philosophical side, doubtless, *In Memoriam* will get antiquated and uninteresting just as Dante's *Divina Commedia* has already to a large extent become ; but the one as well as the other will be read for its beautiful revelations of human feeling, devout longings and spiritual attainment ; and will be ever new as interpreted, in their higher issues, by earnest human lives. The intellectual modes of solving the enigmas of human destiny will change with each succeeding age as they have changed, but in all the changes men will delight to read through these glasses, more darkly or clearly, the struggles of heroic human hearts.

Having said this much my readers will be prepared for this next remark, that a proper appreciation of the spirit out of which *In Memoriam* sprang, and the issues to which it led, is essential to rightly understanding the later works of Tennyson. And yet it is astonishing the remarks one comes upon not only in drawing-rooms but in review-articles, as to this poem. It is still frequently spoken of as the outcome of mere morbid feeling, in a mild whisper, of course; and then again it is vague, cloudy, and obscure, remarks made in a rather bolder key because they appear somewhat more critical. The first remark is so short-sighted as not to be worth notice, and the other is as absurd as the dictum of that critic who pronounced the *White Doe of Rylstone* the worst poem ever imprinted. For who ever heard of philosophers following their problems to the very verge of the Infinite and not being cloudy and obscure? Tennyson struggles with, or touches on the edge of, all these questions and *In Memoriam* partakes generally of the obscurity of the questions he has been dealing with; only this has to be said, that it is constantly relieved and lighted up, as no merely philosophical treatise ever yet was, by deep glances aside at life, religion or friendship. *In Memoriam*, in short, is a picture of the way in which a true soul at last obtains consolation for bereavement—a significant showing forth of the futility of all vain earthly philosophies after due trial has been made of these—a proving, as only such things can be proved, that from each flower of human wisdom the true spirit, as it rises higher, yet reaps a blossom for its brow, as the bee extracts honey from very poison-flowers. We see, too, that as the spirit humbly forms these beautiful flowers into a shade to hide from itself the brightness of the glory it has ventured to approach, the full clear light of heaven breaks through upon it, and as the flower opens its heart to the sun so the deepest human experience flows sweetly forth in music like this :—

> Forgive my grief for one removed,
> Thy creature, whom I found so fair.
> I trust he lives in thee, and there
> I find him worthier to be loved.

And although the being mourned for is no imaginary creature—no half-abstraction, like Milton's *Lycidas*, but a real bosom-friend and college-companion, we find that sorrow gives place to cheerful content, and doubt and discontent,—" ill brethren," yield to a calm determination to live nearer to " that friend who lives in God."

As being perhaps the most direct way of showing the wealth of life our poet has gained, let my readers only realize the meaning of the circumstance of a poet actually praying for forgiveness for writing such a poem. This is surely something new and unprecedented in the annals of poetry. One can scarcely conceive Coleridge, Keats, or Byron—all so proud of the sensuously-beautiful forms in which they clothed their conceptions—doing such a thing. Scarcely even can we think of Shakspeare or Milton establishing such a precedent. " Gentle Will," to be sure, was a puzzling fellow, and had surprising depths of humility and wisdom in him. Little as we know about him, we know this that he was a busy man, and made grand practical use of life. He wrote all these plays and poems, so full of observation and insight, and redolent with wise things, and yet he managed a theatre so well that he made money by it. And managing a theatre, it seems, is no easy piece of work. It has prematurely killed some of the cleverest men of our day by the ceaseless stress and strain it lays upon the mind. But Shakspeare did that prudently, and doubtless had no time to admire his worst self in these productions of his, or to make rhymed complaints about the badness of his lot, and indite " most musical, most melancholy" protests against destiny—so common a fashion with poetic souls. His strange indifference to fame, and his quiet uncomplaining application to his drudgery of theatre-managing, *are* well worth noting, and are, perhaps, as significant as the writing of these wondrous plays of his. Milton, again, is at once relieved and burdened by the consciousness of a direct commission to compose his great poem, and yet, strangely enough, he vastly prefers *Paradise Regained* to the *Paradise Lost.* This fact has also some significance in relation to the point raised here. But Alfred Tennyson says calmly and deliberately, of this glorious poem, *In Memoriam,* so full of knowledge, beauty, and heroic height of mind :—

> Forgive these wild and wandering cries,
>   Confusions of a wasted youth;
>   Forgive them where they fail of truth,
> And in thy wisdom make me wise.

After a verse like that one can readily enough credit

what is sometimes whispered, that Tennyson does not read criticisms on his own poetry. He has learned, in one sense, to be far severer on himself than any other man could possibly be. " Wild wandering cries " and " youthful confusions " are what no critic in his senses would call *In Memoriam;* and yet that is the poet's own last serious verdict upon it. And from his standpoint, which is an infinitely higher one than that of the crowd of critics, that verdict is absolutely true. The preface to the poem in fact supplies the real life-interpretation—the key to all that is obscure and metaphysical in it—throws over it a flood of light in which the " shadows of the mind " disappear and are wholly lost. But that verse we have now quoted is, perhaps, the most significant of the whole. Seldom has such an inspiration visited a poet, and scarcely ever, if it has, has he uttered it with such prophet-like truthfulness and purpose. For while the poet can suffer himself to brood composedly over the outer form of his creation, and can wholly shut out from him life and its duties—the world and its claims—as if his possession of poetic faculty would excuse gross dereliction of common duties, he is actually losing his manhood, and his poethood must soon go when that has gone. The true poet having given shape to his thought, or his fancy, finds no sentimental pleasure in contemplating it—rather turns away with a sigh and hurries forward to realize himself in the highest of all testimonies—giving his thoughts the warm clothing of action, that universal human language, which no one, learned or simple, can possibly misunderstand.

The other mood is a most pitiable one, and can only end in misery; hence the wretched lot of the crowd of so-called poets. Why, is it not this mood of soul which pants for proud solitude and isolation, and seeks to fulfil its highest being by surrounding itself with all beautiful images and artistic forms that our poet himself has so grandly pictured in his *Palace of Art?* There we have a fine, a great soul resolving to live alone unto herself in " her high palace-hall," putting aside common human relations, and scorning union with the common mass for common ends. But her existence soon becomes a most miserable one. The glorious pictures on the walls

> Become uncertain shapes, and, unawares,

She comes

> On white-eyed phantasms, weeping tears of blood,
> And horrible nightmares.

She comes, too, at noon, " On corpses three months old that stood against the wall "—symbols these of beautiful human relations, by her forgotten, and violated in hapless self-worship.

This fine but wretched soul, in her self-sought artistic isolation, has become " a still salt pool, locked in with bars of sand; left on the shore," whose chief misery it is to hear the ceaseless moan and movement of the great ocean of life from which she has unhappily cut herself off. Out of her gloom comes "scorn of herself," and then "laughter at her self-scorn." At the last she rushes forth, to join herself with the common herd she has so despised, and actually to regain her humanity by sympathy and companionship with the commonest and the lowliest.

> " Make me a cottage in the vale," she cried,
>   " Where I may mourn and pray ;
> Yet pull not down my palace towers, that are
>   So lightly, beautifully built :
> Perchance I may return *with others* there
>   When I have purged my guilt."

Mark here the expression "with others." Like the finger-post in a difficult and neglected road, showing that some careful one has traversed the way before us, this little expression directs us and relieves our anxiety. It is full of practical meaning and life-guidance. Perhaps no two words in any modern poem more so. The outward-beautiful — products of the imagination,— art, and its treasures, are to be used in the true sense, with Christian consecration, not for selfish enjoyment or individual aggrandizement in any form, but always with reference to the good of others. And as sorrow itself may even become selfish by being treated artistically, inasmuch as the mind may be drawn from real life-concerns to consume itself in isolated and morbid efforts, so our poet takes care to show that he has abnegated all such forms of inverted pleasure. Art is little and long ; life is great and changeable and short. Such a

testimony to the futility of art and to the grandeur of
life's lowliest relations from the first poet of the day is
the more valuable, because in literature the selfish deifi-
cation of sorrow is one of the commonest phenomena.
Indeed, subjectivity at its base implies the idea of conscious disease or sorrow, and for a poet to be continuously
subjective is to be on the road to scepticism, because its
first result is to teach discontent, and to incapacitate for
the doing of duty. And in this way. The self-conscious
in a mind in any respect worthy the designation of poetic
will be kept alive, stimulated by a constant undercurrent ✓
reference to the mystery and wonder of the Infinite.
Grief, unrest, melancholy solitude, and a diseased self-
worship ultimately, are the children born of this mood
of mind, which, in any nature that will assert itself
true and serenely complete, must be overcome and firmly
renounced. Surely Goethe says well and wisely, "Man
is born not to solve the problem of the universe, but to
find out where the problem begins, and then to restrain
himself within the limits of the comprehensible." In a
word, the subjective in all forms of it is a worship of
self, while divided and diseased; it is a practical denial
of the scriptural maxim, "Look not each man to his own
things, but also to the things of others;" and its ultimate result, if persevered in, is death to true manhood.

Therefore it is that Tennyson, tremblingly afraid that
he may have been wasting too much time and too many
words on a sorrow which was to him what it could be

to no other creature, recalls the reader to his brotherhood with him by showing that all the stores of science
and poetry accumulated in *In Memoriam* are but steps
of a ladder, the end whereof is in the true human
empyrean where all meet and worship the one Father.
In a word, the poet shows, by this unique prayer, that
he has risen into that sphere where religion and poetry
become one; where there is no longer any conflict
between spirit and form ; where the finite and the
infinite are no longer different or divided, but sides of
one reality; where the man and the poet are no longer
separated or at variance, but melt and merge together,
producing thus singleness of eye, heart, mind, and
purpose. And so we can conceive of Tennyson as unlike
the crowd of so-called poets—miserable, vain, ambitious,
self-seeking—rather a noble, contented, industrious,
sympathetic soul.

Some readers would doubtless admire this poem
most for its science—its geology; and others, perhaps,
for its theology, for it contains some of that, too; only
it is said by those who know more about theologians
than the writer of this essay, that they never admire
anything, unless it happens to belong to their own school.
Now Alfred Tennyson, though I hold him one of the
soundest theologians in *In Memoriam* does not link
himself to any school. He belongs not to low church,
nor high church, but to the truly broad human school
of divinity. As to the geology of this poem, let my

readers only think of that verse, and what it contains :—

> O earth, what changes thou hast seen !
> There where the long street roars, hath been
> The stillness of the central sea.

That is really the textlet of all our more recent developments of geological science. And then that passage, too, is a wonderful one which begins :—

> "So careful of the type?" but no.
> From scarped cliff and quarried stone, &c.

It would be the easiest thing in the world to give scores of pieces of sound theology embedded, or rather embalmed, in this poem. If, for instance, any one wanted a refutation of pantheism, as dogmatic as that of an orthodox clergyman, but not on logical grounds ; on those rather of human needs and instincts, he might cite this :—

> That each, who seems a separate whole,
>   Should move his rounds, and fusing all
>   The skirts of self again, should fall
> Remerging on the general soul,
> Is faith as vague as all unsweet:
>   Eternal form shall still divide
>   The eternal soul from all beside ;
> And I shall know him when we meet.
> And we shall sit at endless feast,
>   Enjoying each the other's good:
>   What vaster dream could hit the mood
> Of Love on earth?

Personal recognition in the future is put clearly enough in these lines, one would say. And then, do you want a formal rejection of all vain, vaunting human philosophies—take this, which solves all the difficulties as to the freedom of the will, origin of evil, and such like problems, which lead inevitably to endless mazes of metaphysical obscurity :—

> Our wills are ours, we know not how ;
> Our wills are ours to make them thine.

Do you desire a poet's testimony to the doctrinal truth that there is no merit in man, or man's best deeds—if so, take this :—

> Forgive what seemed my sin in me;
> What seemed my worth since I began ;
> For merit lives from man to man,
> But not from man, O Lord, to thee.

Then if you wish a sentence to prove the relation of reverent fear to love of the Highest, Tennyson has that too :—

> We are fools, and slight;
> We mock thee when we do not fear.

And in these days, when so much is made of merely intellectual education, this verse has a deep practical significance :—

> Let knowledge grow from more to more,
> But more of reverence in us dwell ;
> That mind and soul, according well,
> May make one music as before,
> But vaster.

Tennyson's orthodoxy could never indeed be doubted by any one who read this poem not as a series of dogmatic, or final statements of belief but rather as a sort of philosophical biography—as a description of moods through which the poet passed on his way to the attainment of a certain high spiritual experience.

Properly taken, *In Memoriam* is not poetical in its parts, but only becomes so in its result—in the moral victory which the poet has gained, and which he so significantly tells us of, by actually putting what is really the last portion of the poem first. This may seem paradoxical ; it is true, nevertheless. All that is externally poetical in the body of the poem, simply arises from the manner in which a highly-gifted spirit would relieve itself in the pauses of its grapplings with those purely philosophical problems, which the poet, as a poet, has no right to concern himself about. The origin of evil, the immortality of the soul, the being and personality of God, and recognition in the future state, are not questions the poet has any call, in his own character, to deal with. Yet if these were abstracted from *In Memoriam*, what of the poem would be left? Little or nothing. Whence then, it may well be asked, arise its great beauty and power? I answer, from the moral interpretive, from the deeps of the poet's personality, which he has so suggestively placed at the beginning, and in which he discovers an insight far beyond the superficial paltering criticism that has been devoted to this poem, when he says sincerely of it :—

> Forgive these wild and wandering cries—
> Confusions of a wasted youth.

In Memoriam, in one word, is the philosophical

musings of one whose voice has been formed to rhythm
and can utter itself in no other way—one who has been
stricken into a track of unwonted, and almost unwel-
come contemplation by a great misfortune, and will give
his musings voice for his friends' sake, and that he still
may have a sort of existence in the world. But the
poet feels keenly that the ideas and the form are not
truly accordant with each other, and that they only
become so when he has reached that point at which he
can return with childlike trust to the might of Christ's
teachings, and when he might almost fall back on some
of the sweet, refreshing words of John the Beloved.

There is one composition that has been much read,
quoted, and talked about during the last dozen years,
which is very apt to force itself before the mind, when
speaking of *In Memoriam*. This is the *Festus* of
Bailey. At the imminent risk of seeming to repeat
myself, I make bold to extract a short passage from a
review of this poem written some time ago, as it will
perhaps help to make still clearer my ideas regarding
In Memoriam, and the root of individual experience,
whence springs its genuine poetic character :—

" We deny that *Festus* is a poem, or that it has the
slightest title to be styled dramatic. Notwithstanding
its artistic-seeming dress it is simply a philosophical
scheme of the universe, as abstract and unintelligible as
that of Hegel or Schelling. The difference between it
and *In Memoriam* might be thus expressed :—*In Memo-*

riam, paradoxical as the expression may appear, is not poetical in its parts (for the poet does mean something, when, in these wonderful lines, he so significantly calls it—'wild wandering cries,' and 'confusions of a wasted youth,') but we get evidence of a glorious moral result, in the perfecting and strengthening of the individual will through pain and sorrow; and from the last portion of the poem there falls back, over all the rest, the softening, beautifying light of a rich and blessed experience. *Festus*, on the other hand, if it contains any poetry at all, is poetical only in its parts; as a whole it is a metaphysical chaos, and this simply because the dogma so directly applied in it from beginning to end, has annihilated that true individuality, which has, by Christianity, been brought so clearly to light. There is no sweet uniting element here, arising from the gradual upgrowth of deep spiritual life in the soul of the so-called hero; for, to the last, he is simply a sensuous youth, sated, however, with some forms of pleasure.

" And Tennyson is far truer to the spirit of the great poets Mr. Bailey professed in form to follow, though to supersede in meaning. How clear and real is Job, how individual and direct, and most so in the close of the drama, with his sons and his daughters round him; and his neighbours, because of the demonstration of his worth, bringing each their piece of money, and their earring of gold. And then the supernatural machinery, if we may name it so, is here kept so distinct and distant from the real personages in the drama, only showing itself in its influence on the mind and heart of Job, who, in his worst distress, can pray for his mistaken friends. All is so complete, and we see at once in Job's failings and his greatnesses, that he is a perfect type of the wide human heart at its best. And then to come to far lower ground. Does not Faust, in the second part of Goethe's drama, also show how, as passion is gradually put down, will rises strong, and at length supreme? *Festus* is evidently the production of a man of strong nature, and with a gift of formative power, and some faculty of musical expression; but who, driven into the metaphysical track, has, in the hurry of ideas, over-ridden his poor Pegasus, and killed him out with the very first hot race.

"In *Festus*, instead of the clear, distinct showing forth of the gradual perfection of the individual nature, you have, as we have said, the merging of that almost mechanically into the universal soul, under the name of God. And we cannot help feeling that, if ever it *should* come forth into definite individual life again, it will still have the same puzzling life-problems to meet, because it has never practically mastered them. *Festus*, in fact, ends by an arbitrary metaphysical transformation scene, which suits the dogma of the writer, and gets rid of the difficulty of finding a *denouement* of a different character; but Mr. Bailey has only conveyed his character to a point at which, properly speaking, the poetical might have begun to show itself."

With the view of rendering quite plain the apparently paradoxical statement that *In Memoriam* is not poetical in its parts, it may be remarked that that is the truest poetry which in its last utterance becomes prose—prose in all that simplicity, natural clearness, and uninvolved force which meets us in the very highest efforts of the select few. In reading, say the Old Testament poetry, every one, even the most uncultivated, feels at once that it would be difficult by any feat of measure to render the poetry the least more sublime or impressive. *In Memoriam* also furnishes a beautiful proof of this truth—that the loftier the moral height the singer reaches the purer, more simple, will his expression become, the more will it relieve itself from the extraneous help of special arbitrary forms, and ally itself with ordinary language. It has been thoughtfully pointed out that the earliest poetry is the lyrical, which, strangely enough, is at once the freest in spirit and the most restricted in form ; but that it constantly struggles to merge into the epic, and that again into the broader dramatic. In poetic development, you have thus thought, musical thought if you will, struggling for freer outlet, for an escape from the limitation of the very form which arbitrarily marked it off as poetical at the first. The various subsidiary divisions of poetry may be regarded then as transition phases of poetical thought moving towards an ultimate prose expression. Shakspeare's highest poetry becomes, in fact, mere rhythmic history

with a due infusion of the baldest prose, and that introduced, too, at the very points where formal readers and
critics devoted to the unities would have fancied the
dignity of his subject would most positively have suggested the use of verse. But Shakspeare knew better
than Voltaire and folk of that kidney.

All true poetry thus tends toward prose, and actually
grows the more poetical when it reaches that unrestricted
and familiar form. Of course the idea, the meaning,
may have a deep and subtle circle of relations not easily
caught or fully unfolded even by the most thoughtful;
but there will assuredly be no ambiguity about the words
themselves in their severe simplicity, nor about that
outer sphere of significancy which all at first alike seek
to appropriate. Poetry of the genuine order is like the
ancient Jewish temple : it has its outer court into which
all may come, and its inner court or 'holiest' into which
only the select or the "trusted" are or can be admitted.
Poetry, to the end, will thus be essentially mystical—one
of what Novalis has called the "select things." Though
it will present a series of pictures or symbols in which
the actual facts of life are embodied, yet these facts
themselves are again but symbols of spiritual facts and
laws. Job may be read purely as a disproving of the
narrow dogma of the Jews, that he who was afflicted
suffered for his own or his parents' sins. Hamlet may
be regarded as an excellent representation of the notion
of filial revenge as at one time held to be a duty. But

those would be but poor interpretations, though, doubtless, in one point of view, legitimate. We find the same double lesson in Homer, *Prometheus*, the *Divina Commedia*, the *Pilgrim's Progress*, the *Palace of Art*, *In Memoriam*, and *Paracelsus*. All these, on that very account, are mystical in the better sense of that word.

But what, my readers may ask, is the mystical? We have been accustomed, they may say, to regard it as certainly signifying nothing good, and now you perplex us by actually applying the term to the world's masterpieces. I will tell shortly what mysticism in the bad sense is, and then my readers may, perhaps, manage to discover by contrast what the other or good sort is. Bad mysticism, then, may arise in either of two ways. The intense force of the spiritual conception may make a man withdraw himself from men to such a degree that he actually loses hold on their language and habits, the sphere of nature and social forms melts before him into an impalpable unreality, retiring into the distance like summer thunder-clouds before the blinding sunlight. The consequence is that we have vague, incoherent, unsatisfactory renderings, though the meaning itself may be deep, genuine, earnest; and this simply because the symbol is not accordant with fact—unnatural, misty, and undefined. We see this in Jacob Boehme, sometimes, too, in Novalis.

The highest idealist is the thorough realist. In this sense it may be said, that he always shows himself in accord with nature, and his form drawn directly from her, is characteristic of her—calm, simple, defined, complete. But mysticism in the bad sense may spring from the too-determinate linking of the spiritual with a series of individual external appearances, so that there is no unity in the relation of the symbols, each standing out apart and cold, while the whole has a cramped, hampered, artificial, and contradictory aspect. This we have in Swedenborg, sometimes, we regret to say, in thoughtful Robert Browning, and notably in the earlier works of the gifted George MacDonald. Indeed, the last-named writer affords the most striking illustration that could almost be given of an advance from doubtful mysticism to true poetry. *Phantastes*, how cramped, arbitrary, and unnatural! *David Elginbrod*, again, how spiritual, natural, and abounding in subtle meanings and suggestions! As a work of fiction, this last is very truthful and honest; the characters and outer incidents of the poem (for it is actually a poem) are as clear, real, and true as those of Thackeray himself. *David Elginbrod* is the work of a genuine mystic—a man who believes in the infinite as present, as existing not far away and in the future; but close beside us, in us, and upholding us constantly. There is great natural clearness in the work; and it has consequently remarkable depth and breadth. The world from the lowliest to the loftiest is but a window through which an inner sphere of life and marvel is reflected upon us. With

Mr. MacDonald as with all true poets there has ceased
to exist any actual separation as between seen and
unseen, physical and spiritual; and his works are
earnest attempts to bring men and women to practically
realize and live under this belief. The poor idiot
"Cornel" in the *Wow o' Riven* lives very near to the
infinite—the church bell revealing the very highest
to him—is in fact, the little window through which his
darkened soul can yet read the eternal. Though he has
no more articulate message his faith fails not; the bell
does for him what our Bibles sometimes fail to do for
us—keeps him in active hope of being taken "hame."
David Elginbrod and the *Bell* are as truly poems in all
the essential requisites of poetry as the most elaborate
of our nineteenth century rhymes.*

In Memoriam also belongs to this category inasmuch
as it becomes the more truly poetical the more the poet
seems to escape from the strict conditions of his measure,
breaks it up and makes it next neighbour to prose. For
it is assuredly a sin in the poet to put his purest,
noblest in a form that will first charm the sense, and
may never accomplish aught more. Tennyson has
deeply felt this and has given expression to it in the
most memorable of words; and therefore one need not

---

* Indeed were I here and now to make bold to tender a solemn
brotherly advice to such a pure aspiring soul as Mr. MacDonald I would
say in all seriousness—never rhyme again; and if the materials for an
idyll do gather about you, then throw them into just such a shape as
The Bell.

wonder that some shallow-minded people should read his later books for fashion's sake, and mildly iterate the opinion that he ·has declined because he paints less gorgeously and sensuously in *Enoch Arden* than in *Locksley Hall* or *Œnone* ; now-a-days apparently playing tricks in writing blank verse that sometimes seems little other than masterly musical prose. It is nevertheless because the first proof of his having attained this height is seen in *In Memoriam* that I have placed it so immeasurably above all the poems which have been dictated by like feelings and circumstances. If any one only reads thoughtfully the sections beginning with the lines, " Sad Hesper o'er the buried sun," and " Though truths in manhood darkly join "—both so beautiful in sentiment and expression from a certain point of view ;— and takes the trouble to compare these carefully with the direct, simple, sharply-defined conclusiveness of each line in the preface he will soon I humbly think discover my meaning in this. Here there is far-reaching stretch of thought, one would say; but the deepest thought become intensely practical and living. Emerson says somewhere that " the inmost becomes in due time the outmost." The eternal thoughts of God become a world made up of laws of gravitation and other like elements ; but God himself becomes a little child in the very furthest sphere of his many worlds. And to descend a step : the holiest thoughts of man must be broken on the wheel and at last take the outermost, commonest and lowliest garb of language. It is a principle this which goes deep. The highest in spirit takes the simplest and commonest form. So at last Tennyson's rhymes in *In Memoriam* become almost prosaic ; because he has risen to sublimer heights of experience than he set out with. He utters faithfully the loftiest thought he has reached and it is essentially a condemning of the spirit out of which the mass of much-admired poetry is written —a putting away from him for ever of that fatal worship of sensuous words and images which are the stock-in-trade of those who are poets only in "circumstance" and nothing more. Intellect with Tennyson is at length submissive to faith, patience, reverence and hope—the man is lost in the child again ; poetry is true childhood's broken, faltering yet reverent utterance and here in these last lines of *In Memoriam* we have it once more sweet, captivating, strong and pure. As the child because he has not yet consciously infringed any law, lives above law in clear translucency of life, moving in a sphere of harmony—of poetry ; so law is actually maintained by some men living above it in the world, being truly a law unto themselves, and thus realizing a veritable sainthood or sacred childhood and speaking not so much harmo niously as speaking truthfully in virtue of a harmony which is lived. In this way poetic life fulfils itself in the few, who thus become essentially independent of all circumstances, forms of rhyme among the rest, and yet they elevate even these while seeming to put them under their feet.

Hence it is perhaps that Thomas Carlyle, a man of vivid insight and intensely practical nature, so hates all verbal jingling and mere rhyming as he does. May it not be because in his view of it the crowd of poets so called are perhaps of all men the furthest from having accomplished that inward victory, by which at last modes of expression are made subservient. According to him they are still fighting vainly for an arbitrary clearness to be derived from trick of words (and are thus worse than wasting valuable time), instead of engaging in real work by which alone wholeness of being, satisfaction, or in other words harmony, might be gained. When, therefore, Carlyle says, that a man should express his idea in prose, if he can at all, in preference to rhyme, he, in his own characteristically rugged, informal but practical way, applies this great principle. He simply means that a man should keep his idea or fancy till it has become part and parcel of his life, and made music there; and when that is accomplished, the expression will be poetical, it matters not whether it be rhyme or prose. In short, that is only poetic with Carlyle, which derives all its poetry from the spirit, and is perfectly independent of words and their arrangements, which is not poetical merely in its parts and dress, but in the whole and as a whole.

And here it might well be asked, what right have young people to begin limning certain isolated passages of human experience in the very style and manner they have so often been before, when they have no power to show, and indeed no right to try to show, the development of those into purer moods, and their relation to that healthy up-growth which, as I understand it, is the one thing these dark and morbid elements exist to develop, so far at all events as poetry is concerned? Individual and isolated moods of a morbid and diseased character have no more right to be painted by themselves, and for the sake of showing skill in the use of words, than have certain necessary processes of nature to be performed in public. Does not nature carefully shroud her roots down amid stench and dung and rotting leaves of former years, and wait patiently till she gets her fruit in preparation before she gives any visible evidence of her secret processes? So likewise should poetical writers with a vast deal of the morbid sentimental experiences now boldly written of. They should wait, like nature, till the dung of life has nurtured the tree of will into beautiful blossom, and then their presenting us with a sprig may be at once pleasant and profitable. As for the other it produces nausea, and ought to be everywhere proscribed and mercilessly put down. Says Goethe wisely, "there are some things which, though known to all, should yet be treated as secrets, because it works on modesty and good morals." Our rhymers should consider this. They are not without an exemplar even in the dress and circumstances of the present which they also fight with. Let them look how wonderfully Alfred

Tennyson excuses and justifies his dealing with these moods by faithfully exhibiting the life-flower that has grown out of them. Let them examine thoughtfully the end of *Locksley Hall* first of all, then the close of *Maud*, the introduction to *In Memoriam* next, and last *Enoch Arden*, and I think they will at once see what is meant here.

But indeed that blind rush and whirl of sensuous high-sounding phrases so usual with young poets, only proves too clearly their entire want of claim to speak at all. It signifies that to their eyes all is yet new and strange. To the true poet nothing is new; rather all the wonder of the universe has become common. He has made his home in it, and is no more distracted by the changing, uncertain, and strikingly arbitrary aspect of much that surrounds him. He has got the key; the secret is opened up to him and calmly he can instruct, and lead, and delight by kindly elevating. He needs no trick of words to help out his meaning, but in simplest guise gives us the forecast of truths as if they had from of old been his daily familiars.

It is a perception of these truths acting on a nature peculiarly keen and subtle, and yet with a twist or irregularity running through it, that has made Robert Browning adopt that strange puzzling form, half-verse, half-prose, especially in some of his more distinctly lyrical pieces. He is determined that no one shall accept him as a poet simply because of smooth or finished lines, and yet so self-consciously does he thrust his idea from him that the ordinary reader of poetry, or one who had formed his notion of what poetry ought to be from Pope's rhymes, or critics of the Jeffrey school, would most assuredly be at first repelled. Yet Browning has attained great richness of experience—harmony of thought and life. He has advanced upon it, however, by peculiar and exceptional pathways, which have left upon him marks that go to indicate an eccentric personality. Reading his poetry is like hearing Shakspeare acted in a German theatre—you are drawn to him one moment by something English, and the next again repelled by something foreign. He writes like a man who has forgotten the simple speech of his childhood, and preserved in remembrance only its vaguest philosophical vocabulary. And yet he is not a philosopher; indeed he but too clearly keeps before the reader his revolt against metaphysical thought in all the phases of it. But notwithstanding those things, there are sometimes such sweet, rich, fragrantly natural bursts that we are reminded of violets among honey. Browning has not, like Tennyson, studied as an artist the resources of his mother-tongue, and though he can express himself with great power occasionally, he has not added that grace and charm which always accompany simplicity. So far as fixing our poetic forms is concerned, *In Memoriam* will have far more influence than *Paracelsus* or *Dramatis Personæ*, or indeed all the works of Browning put together; and the reason simply is that Tennyson has held more by the clear, the old, the universal, the simple.

There is still another consideration which would help us to a proper contrast of these our two greatest living poets. Schiller, in one of his essays, says that the true literary man should be like the son of Agamemnon, "dreadful to purify;" but yet that he should elevate the men of his time by showing how a truly earnest spirit can consecrate and ennoble any form whatsoever. The artist is to take for his forms those which are received by his age. He is to breathe a new life into them, and so purify while seeming to accept. Such a work without any complaining or self-conscious boasting did William Shakspeare. Though hampered, not only by arbitrary rules, but by the filthy degrading tastes of his time, he yet was on the whole pure, and has written some poems which will live for ever. No good can come of railing—of continual complaint and protest. It is better to fight quietly for the good than to rail loudly at the ill. Mr. Browning's poems are, in their form, a continuous and angry protest against his age, its ideas, its habits. He feels that he does well to be angry. So far, however, as this spirit is felt to be present with the poet in his work, the unity of purpose is marred, and the effect is weakened. Tennyson, we believe, feels all this as intensely as does Browning. But he has not, on that account, felt himself justified in showering con-

tempt broadcast on his neighbours; he has quietly
worked on, sometimes, perhaps in sorrow to give his
poems that graceful roundedness of finish, simply that
he might form a fitting pathway for the truth he has
been sent to proclaim. He has not complained or pro-
tested—nay, he has sometimes, in the quietest manner
possible, warned the critics, could they have taken
warning, by afterwards altering his poems in such a way
as to make the gifted fraternity declare that the verbal
rhythm has been marred? Often by these little modi-
fications Tennyson shows that he feels all that Robert
Browning has been so perplexed by, and asserts his
superiority over him, inasmuch simply as he quietly
stoops down, and without reproach, though much against
his desire, makes for himself a lowly way of entrance to
the soul and heart of his own century.

Mystical as may seem this idea of mine as to prose
being the ultimate and highest form of poetic utterance,
it is not so very unnatural after all. Philologists tell
us that the earliest utterances of man are a sort of verse,
and that the grand attainment, to which the rude primitive versification is but the preparation, is the power of
clear and forcible prose expression. Coleridge somewhere speaks of the pleasurable surprise that would be
felt by an early people accustomed to rudely modulated
songs, when some one first struck into the sphere of prose
and ruled it grandly. And what more likely or consistent than that the same course should be followed in the

development of poetry—that poetic forms should at their highest lose themselves in beautiful flowing prose. Why may not the poet be called to obey that same rule which we have so good reason for believing humanity itself obeyed and obeys?   There are, however, deeper reasons than this, some of which have been hinted at rather than fully deduced. These reflections are germane to the theme in hand.   In *In Memoriam* rightly studied, we discover at once a progress backward and forward—backward in an approach to the simplicity of the prose form, forward to that calm spirituality and fulness of repose, which being once attained by a man, it may then be truly said that with him "poetry and prose are no longer at variance."

So much for *In Memoriam*, which I sincerely feel unable to praise sufficiently, even worthily.   It is withal so human, so deep, so full of tender clinging affection. All through the clouds of philosophy there break such rays of faith, hope, and triumph.   Its conclusion melts into a psalm—a psalm sung with some of our later accompaniments, such as David knew not of.   If it hints at doubts, despairs, as David's psalms hint so often of dark sins in thought and deed, does not love always clear that away again, and brighten the background the more into beauty, as a seamed, scarred, careworn face looks grander than another, when it smiles softly upon us through traces of suppressed tears?

And let no reader for a moment fancy that in the

last paragraph, I daringly pulled in the name of the sweet singer of Israel merely for a rhetorical turn. I know well that the Psalms of David are by far the most perfect of lyrical poems; but in our hasty superficial formalism we have almost forgot the true, human way to read these, and actually need *In Memoriams* to help us back to fresh insight. For, let any man of the least openness of soul and independent strength of mind, take the Book of Psalms, and beginning with the first, let him read on and ask himself when he comes to the opening of the third, whether there is not there an entire change of note. The fact is, that as Goethe and Bailey have each in the openings of their dramas afar off followed Job, and then in the body of the poem attempted to vary the ideas, and even the form, to suit the time, so Tennyson, all unconsciously, and simply, I believe, because he had risen to a certain height of poetic experience, has followed David, even in form, in exhibiting his trials—"defects of doubt, and taints of blood"—and what he gained by them. As you have the grand practical result in the preface to *In Memoriam*, so the first two Psalms are the gathering up in true words of David's triumph—a fitting expression of what David had learned through all the varied contradictory experiences of the more than a hundred lyrics that went before. The first Psalm—properly the first of the last two—simply expresses the writer's absolute faith in right, in personal purity, and the consequent harmony of

9

the individual will, with its resultant blessedness. The second again reflects the same principle only in relation to states; indicating their duty towards those truths which, faithfully adhered to by a people, will lead to *real* prosperity and permanence, because their efforts will be sanctioned by God and the universe. Then the third properly begins the lyrical journey—the mystical auto-biography throughout telling of the highest, hinting truly at the lowest and weakest—how the soul rises falls, sins aspires, doubts trusts; and how at last, as the poem comes near the close, the whole being gathers itself up into a full-flowing diapason of praise. And so also in its measure, and in its own way does *In Memoriam.* Ours is a philosophical, divided, pre-eminently a doubting time—a hasty, impetuous, fevered time indeed, when even men's bloods are tainted by the falsenesses and the ghoulish appetites of their fathers; and so Tennyson does in his own way for us what David did for his people—shows us how to over-come these peculiarly national and degrading sins, because he himself has wrestled with them and con-quered. And like David, he too points us back once more to childlike trustfulness and reverence and fear.

But to return to Tennyson's properly passionate or love poems, which, in point of time, might have been noticed prior to *In Memoriam.* As, however, they are one and all but partial renderings of the same truth as is more com-pletely wrought out in that great poem, they will perhaps just as fitly be noticed here. They show, in fact, the very same spirit developing itself through the various play of the passion of love, as by the sorrows of friendship in the other. The disappointments and sufferings under both love and friendship minister to the same result on the individual character, to develope and to broaden the will. *Locksley Hall* is the first really worthy poem of this class, and it is great, not so much, perhaps, for the fine thought that plays throughout, and the wonderful command over words, as because the poet in being true to his own experience here at the risk even of artistic incompleteness, has enunciated a great principle, and also suggested rich possibilities, some of which we now joyously regard as realized. In *Locksley Hall* we have a hero who has grappled with his passion and his grief, and puts them beneath him; but who has not yet learned, in the Goethean phrase, "even to love and honour suffering and sorrow, and to look on them not as hindrances, but as having been helps to what is holy." The crushed spirit we see has recovered from its worst writhings, and grimly fronts the sky, *manlike*, rejoicing that it can venture forth to find comfort in some form of activity away from the scene of its wrongs and poignant sorrows. Upon the hero's scathed heart dawns the glory of a great moral truth, that though the individual withers under limitation and wrong, the world still progresses, and that the way to recover health and strength, is to unite with the great advancing phalanx which is ever increasing. By self-denial,—as yet, however strangely enough, gendered mainly by a reaction from passionate self-indulgence—he resolves to regain what has been lost to him of life and its blessings. But still he can in a way curse *Locksley Hall*, and its memories. The poet has here carried the poem to the strict limit of his experience at the time it was written. It closes, but does not cease. It abounds with suggestions as to a higher result in prospect. It points to a region of lofty possibility. In one respect, however, it was unsafe for the poet to leave his hero here; that is, when viewed simply from the formally moral stand-point, which requires that a direct lesson be drawn from everything. If, however, the poet ever again wrote on a kindred theme, it would test at once his insight and fuller experience,—whether he would conduct his hero to a more worthy goal.

In *Maud*, therefore, where we have substantially the same hero as in *Locksley Hall*,—only with the merest touch of finer, more sensitive, and musically strung nature ; and by consequence the deeper possibilities of morbidity,—a still higher note is gained. Here, after all the enjoyment and the hope, that springs out of a true affection, tenderly reciprocated, has been blasted—after untold sufferings, because of the sins and stupidities of others—after madness even, and all its fearful attendant evils the hero awakens to the nobler purpose. And in *Maud* we have, so to speak, all the circumstantialities heightened as against this result being attained. Not only have we here a nature less likely, owing to his early misanthropy, to seek a channel of healthy development in action with his fellows for great ends ; but he has not that relief of deadening satisfaction, if one might name it so, which might be supposed to spring from the knowledge that one who was loved and reverenced had declined below his level so unworthily, as in *Locksley Hall.* The hero here has to face the shadow of Maud's constancy wherever he moves, and carries it about with him as a dark-bright something to set against the meannesses and brutal rudeness of her friends. With a littler soul, or one less deeply though unconsciously related to the subtle and elevating influences of Christianity, that fact would have made the end attained in this poem almost impossible. But the hero thus far more deeply wronged than he of *Locksley Hall*, yet rises to the sublimest height of soul—becomes almost *Godlike*, because he awakens, as he himself beautifully ends the poem by saying, to the Christian mind :—

And myself have awaked, as it seems, to the better mind ;
It is better to fight for the good, than to rail at the ill ;
I have felt with my native land, I am one with my kind ;
I embrace the purpose of God, and the doom assigned.

In these few lines, simple as they are, notice the wonderful truthfulness of expression—how gradually, as if sharply correspondent with experience, the sphere of life's harmonious fulfilment rounds itself off into completeness. "I have felt with my native land" comes first, indicating the range of political relations, of patriotism, of duty full and faithful to that which lies nearest, most neighbourly. And then again the clause, " I am one with my kind," indicating the sphere of benevolence or wide brotherhood—that lofty and vital impulse which, having for its base the near and the real, can never degenerate into vague, unmeaning, abstract sentimentalism. Then, as if returning upon itself, the soul finds in complete self-abnegation the crown of all this; and hence naturally follows the line, " I embrace the purpose of God, and the doom assigned." Acknowledging thus clearly the absolute goodness of God's ways in a better than merely abstract, English-Church-Prayer-book way, the hero shows how out of what might have seemed superficially a curse has sprung the one crowning glory of life. All the various duties, from lowest to highest, are to be performed and with reverence, because they afford channels for the outgo of the purified being; even as the perfection or fruit-bearing power of the tree, arises from its roots perpetually urging themselves further and deeper into the earth, to meet and appropriate the subtle influences of air and rain.

Maud has been criticized as a light love-poem and as a temporary war-poem. Very superficially, in both instances. Maud is the true " Life-drama" of the period. Here we have all the elements of genuine tragedy, and these, too, so developed as to justify our calling it a

dramatic poem. It is dramatic—not in its form, but in
very spirit and essence. Man, in contact with " Circumstance" or Fate, as of old, is the theme. The hero
inherits more than a morbid predisposition ; he has a
curse—the external expression of that—sent down to
him ; and his nearest neighbours are bound up closely
with him in that curse. His father has speculated, and
been ruined, chiefly through the grasping greed of
Maud's father, and in despair he dashes out his own
life. The hollow where the body was found among the
lichened boulders haunts the memory of the youth, let
him go where he will. External circumstances thus
heavily oppress a mind only too naturally predisposed
to melancholy, and they tend to develop an intensely
morbid state of feeling. The youth broods over wrongs ;
and, as is always the case, creates some imaginary ones
in his morbid musings. Maud comes on the scene at a
perilous moment. The sight of her face will either
educe or deaden for ever his possibilities of fruitful manhood. Long unknown to either, save in dreamiest
recollection of the lad, they two have been betrothed
when the young man was but a child, and Maud
as yet unborn. The fathers have themselves, " over
their wine," forged the fates of their children, and in
the unconscious yet shadowy following of those destinies
of theirs, they precipitate their doom. Maud's brother
has been taught to hate the hero, who now is Maud's
accepted lover. The brother, one night after a ball,

finds the two together not far from the fateful hollow, and upbraids and insults Maud's now doubly-betrothed one. Blows are exchanged. Maud's brother is wounded, possibly killed, and her lover has to flee. Maud soon after dies of grief and shame; while her lover, in a foreign land, frets in misery, till madness, like a tropical tornado, drives out the fevered heat of life, and he emerges a strong man, with will purified and braced to action, for which he calmly, earnestly consecrates himself as for a sacrament. The skill with which the fateful relation of the young lovers is made at last to yield an upas-crop of frightful chastisements for those who made themselves inheritors of the wrong by being perpetuators of the hate, is Shakspearean in its severe truthfulness; and the constant and obtrusive contact of the elements of will and fate is equally impressive and true. But *Maud* is more a Christian poem than *Hamlet*, in so far as the results upon the individual mind and heart of the hero are such as Maud or Ophelia either would have gladly died to have procured for him she loved.

Maud is like the Shakspearean drama in this, that it is universal, and, though it seems to narrow itself to a special period, yet really borrows nothing from anything ephemeral or even historical in the ordinary sense. The Crimean war has really no place in it; though the poet, because the poem was published when men were turning to " the north, and battle, and seas of death," stooped down to a passing circumstance the better, so to speak, to attach his poem to the day. But it is, as a drama of life and as such I persist in viewing it, perfectly independent of all these references. All that is in any respect temporary could be withdrawn, and yet the soul of *Maud* remain untouched. The war mentioned in the poem signifies simply the active opposition to some form of life or power into which it is needful for such a character as the hero at a certain point to throw himself to insure the healthful development of the individual being. "The poet," says Goethe, "as a man and a citizen, will love his native land; but the native land of his *poetic* powers and *poetic* action is the good, noble, and beautiful, which is confined to no particular province or country, and which he seizes upon and forms wherever he finds them. Therein he is like the eagle, who hovers with free gaze over whole countries, and to whom it is of no consequence whether the hare on which he pounces is running in Prussia or in Saxony." This is as true of the part the Crimean war holds in *Maud*, as it could possibly be of anything in any poem whatever.

The works of such an one as Tennyson are mutually interpretive. We have the whole meaning of *Maud*, in its latter part, gathered up in some few lines from a beautiful little poem called *The Islet*, published along with *Enoch Arden*. In this poem the "sweet little wife of the singer" urges him to go with her "for a score of sweet little summers or so" to the ideal,—

"a sweet little Eden on earth that I know." He
replies :—

> No, no, no !
> For in all that exquisite isle, my dear,
>   There is but one bird with a musical throat ;
>   And his compass is but of a single note ;
> That it makes one weary to hear.
>
> No, love, no !
> For the bud ever breaks into bloom on the tree,
> And a storm never wakes on the lonely sea,
>   And a worm is there in the lonely wood,
>   That pierces the liver and blackens the blood,
> And makes it a sorrow to be.

The whole matter lies calmly clear in these words.
They embody the idea which from first to last pervades
Maud, and that poem will never be fully understood
until this idea is definitely seized. " Man," says
Tennyson, " exists to act, and only in stubborn and
persistent action with others for others' good can that
which is best and loftiest be developed in him." In
Maud we have a graceful and complete pictorial rendering
of this truth.

But *Maud* simple as it is when viewed thus, has
been a perfect puzzle to the critics. I have even met
with statements to the effect that this overwrought
rendering of diseased morbidity and that other were in
" the Maud temper," which at least one sapient critic
informed us signified the " misanthropic musings of a
lonely mouse." How sage and deep and wise and

searching the remark! Could the intellectual critic not see that the object of the poem was to show, in the first place, how a solitary, susceptible, over-sensitive being who shunned the crowd not " pleased with the joy of his own thoughts," but haunted and made miserable by scornfully contemptuous thoughts of selfishness and meanness and wrong is yet, almost in opposition to his own long-nursed feelings, led out of himself by the gentle face of one whom to see was to love, and the suddenness of whose appearance, making it impossible for him to escape or call in the aid of reason, accounts for the strange contradictions of his first words regarding her? And did it not appear to him that in the next place Maud shows how that when love had fairly redeemed our hero from the curse of his isolation and morbid scorn, and reunited him to life and all its beautiful healthfulness, that this very love is fatefully crushed, not in itself, that were impossible, but in its circumstances, so that the hero has to atone by sad and weary separation for a deed which every generous reader at once can justify on the ground of the youth's brave spirit, his scant knowledge of men, and his strangeness to all the restraints of society? And could the critic not see further, and most important of all, that these phases of experience running on even into madness itself are all painted with such care and skill simply for the sake of showing that in one way they become servants to the higher and nobler—that by the might of will they can be trans-

muted into blessings and made the root not of individual enjoyment, which would probably have been the
result had the course of love been here supposed to
run smooth, but bounteous gains for the nation who
reared the hero, and even for the world, because through
all these sufferings and sorrows he is helped to his
true inheritance of manhood and, by self-renunciation,
enters the narrow gate on what Sir Thomas Browne
quaintly calls the "asperous way" of life;—becoming
thus too a pattern for one and all of us, who in some
form or other are struggling with the evils and the
difficulties here so cunningly and almost perfectly
symbolized? The closing portion so simple and quietly
grand cannot really be too often quoted, for till the
spirit out of which these lines were written is appropriated and appreciated the poem is not and cannot be
fully understood :—

> We have proved we have hearts in a cause, we are noble still,
> And myself have awaked, as it seems, to the better mind ;
> It is better to fight for the good, than to rail at the ill ;
> I have felt with my native land, I am one with my kind ;
> I embrace the purpose of God and the doom assigned.

And in embracing, like a true Christian, his dark doom
it ceases for ever to be a doom or dark for him; he is
free, joyously realising the fulness of his being; dark
necessity or "circumstance" has no longer any power
over him, and the world itself is on his side to fight for
him and uphold him even should he die in the midst of
his years.

Here at length, in the close of *Maud*, so often criticized merely as a light love-poem, the poet has reached the essential spirit of poetry, and sets to music in words as it has already set his own life to music with itself, that principle which is at once the root of true religion and true poetry. It is from these almost prosaic-seeming lines that the consecrating light is thrown over all that went before, making the morbid discords at last join with higher notes, and merging thus they melt into the subtlest, sublimest music. For as self-denial—that lofty resolution to suffer personal losses and wrongs for the good of others—is the fundamental element in religion, so also is the perception of its beauty and the exhibiting of its triumphs through manifold trials, the business of true poetry. And much as the fact is forgotten it is because that idea, dimly it is true yet far more clearly than in most modern poems, burns through the fleshly figures of Homer's epic that the poem lives and to this day delights crowds of men. Homer's heroes are valiant; that is, they deny themselves and fight for what mirrored itself to them as the Right, the Beautiful. Woman, seduced and wronged, has always been a favourite symbol; it is so even in Christian times; and because in a far-off way Homer truly anticipated chivalry his poem has not been wholly superseded by the poetry of chivalry and later romance. The two are connected and will interpret each other. Old

Greek legends and later Christian ones are in one sense symphronistic. They are so because, though different in forms and incidents, they yet struggle to interpret the same idea; round the same soul they but gather a different garment. And that soul is self-denial, which all poems that humanity has consented to cherish, have consecrated and beautified and made holy.

Through a thousand forms this principle has been reflected, for there is indeed a sublime stretch from a *Prometheus* to a *Pilgrim's Progress;* but where there is no notion of this, but a merely idle decoration of vain conceited fancies, there is no poetry, let the lines be never so musical and skilfully measured. Said John Milton,—"He who would write heroic poems must make his life a heroic poem," which remark if well considered will show the relation of all genuine poetry to Him whom we worship. The *Cottar's Saturday Night* shows how Scotia's laureate was touched into reverence for a purity and beauty of life he aspired after but never really attained. What was grandest in the poet came out in that calmly-joyful Christian picture, which will live notwithstanding the outcry of a certain class against Burns; and that simply because it sprang from the eternal. Can my readers now see the relation of these remarks to *Maud?* It, too, was written out of a heroic experience—a deep Christian sympathy, and with a pure and lofty purpose, though with no conventional moral object; and it but too plainly exhibits the frightfully artificial and false character of our prevailing criticism that the true meaning of *Maud* and its relation to Tennyson's life-scheme have never before been definitely indicated.

But if in *Maud* these great truths may have been only stated dimly, and to a certain extent indirectly, they are unmistakeably the very burden of *Enoch Arden.* The characters here are chosen from the humblest walk of life, and the heroic devotion of the fisherman certainly contrasts well with the sensualism and bravado of a set of poetical heroes now happily out of date and mostly shuffled underground. The incidents of the poem in themselves and taken separately are of the simplest, and they borrow nothing from adventitious trickery of verse, though to be sure the verse is powerful because of its sweet crystalline simplicity and still-flowing clearness. But there is no waste of words, no overheaping of images as we find is the tendency of some of the laureate's imitators, who exaggerate into vulgar over-colouring what with him has always been kept within very strict limits. The harmony of the verse, too, is sometimes broken in on by what seems at first sight little else than intentional irregularity and harshness. Fine as some of the individual lines are, we do not have that long and full-sustained polish which marked his earliest efforts in blank-verse, as for instance in *Œnone* and the *Gardener's Daughter.* On this account we need not be surprised that some of the humorous weeklies, in parodying the poem pronounced many of the lines unscannable. But there it stands, the masterpiece of the age,—so natural and yet so spiritual; so simple and yet so deep and inexhaustible; so subtle and rich in suggestions and yet so perfectly clear and uninvolved. It is as yet the poem of the period, and one knows not where to look even for a second to it.

Tennyson let me say once more is not a mere erratic singer, making his best points by a sort of knack or happy chance. His poems are essentially wholes, although at first glance it might sometimes seem that in the mere form there are breaks or incompletenesses. Yet in a deeper view even these are found by suggestion to express his meaning better than more definite lines could have done. As a conscientious practical builder does not seek after an absolutely perfect wall, and yet simply in his desire to do a workmanlike thing, unconsciously exhibits and applies the deepest laws, so a man like Tennyson. Great truths will be found lying half-hidden under the most commonplace passages, and when they are brought together and studied a unity will be found to pervade them, as in nature we see that remote things have a relation to those nearer and more familiar, and are even closely dependent on them. A truth this which Novalis expresses beautifully, when he says of one of his pupils at Sais,—"soon he no more saw anything alone; men, stars, clouds, and flowers spoke to each other, and he rejoiced to bring them together."

If then we take one or two of the separate and indeed somewhat confusing incidents in *Enoch Arden*, as viewed from a conventional point of view, we may find some proof of this truth. The very first feeling that arises upon a careful reader is a sort of oppressive fatefulness, which only completely clears away with the latter portion of the poem, if to some minds it would do so even then. This arises from the fact that there plays through it a series of coincidences, which indeed only become possible in poetry by a seeming disregard for certain arbitrary moral forms. Every one who would read *Enoch Arden* truly must discover the relation which, with the poet, conventional laws hold to the spirit of morality—how that the latter may even be perfected into the loftiest spirituality by the apparent or circumstantial infringement of the former. Enoch Arden's history indeed becomes romantic at the very point this begins to appear, and where first of all those strangely-fateful coincidences which, with a less thoroughly Christian man, would have typed the existence of some relentless Fate like that of the ancients, begin to thrust themselves forward into prominence. The after-lot of the characters is fore-shadowed in their youthful pastimes—as woman and as girl Annie is little wife to both; the very anxiety and care of Enoch become the causes of that which broke his heart, while again in the self-same hollow where Enoch and Annie in sight of Philip first kiss each other, Philip himself at the moment forgetful, makes proffer of marriage to Annie more than ten years afterwards; the reverie of Enoch on his solitary island is broken in on by the peal of marriage-bells, and Annie for a whole year after a union she could no longer delay, is haunted habitually by the shadow of Enoch. And yet as can be shown the feeling of a blind mocking relentless Fate having power in human affairs, disappears in the light of Duty, just as the shadows of morning melt in the brightness of the awakening day; and we are thus only made to feel the more the deep significancy of seeming-little things, and how a valiant simple Christian faith cannot be shaken by these, but only strengthened and intensified. Thus it is that each line opens up into new vistas of thought and meaning, while yet the individual incidents and the outer construction of the poem are so simple, that the youngest boy or girl might understand and muse over it with unqualified satisfaction and delight, as at some grandly daring action which had its impulse in affection or self-denial.

With a French novelist, or for that part even an English one, the story, as in *Lady Audley*, would have developed into two or three murders and a suicide. But how beautifully Tennyson's deeper perception of Christianity comes in, spreading a cheering steady light through it all, and lifting, as it were, the very frailties and blindnesses of humanity into strengths and beauties. Well has it been said that all that truly pertains to poetry in a Christian time must spring from Jesus, for he is "the centre of every possible modern epic," the hero being a hero in virtue of the light thrown upon his character from that ever-living source of goodness. Tennyson's poem answers fully to the requirement, and makes us feel how much grander and richer is human life than we are often apt to take it for.

Enoch Arden has been called a "melancholy tale." I can hardly agree with that judgment. It is quite true that under what one may call the classical rôle melancholy memories of strangely-fateful and gloomily-suggestive coincidences would have been borne in upon the mind and heart of the hero in such circumstances as he at the last finds himself. Nay, he might actually have been brought to feel as if a fearful bond had been woven round him in regard to which he was so helpless that he could only sit down and brood passively over his misery—a man chained to an isolated rock with horrid hateful memories, like eagle beaks, gradually plucking out his life, as the vultures indeed were fabled to have plucked at the heart of Prometheus while he lay bound to his cliff, and bore with stoical patience the sad mockery of his fate. It was in this way only that the classical artists could construe the action of free-will. Its grandest out-go with them was a desperate struggle to *bear* rather than to *do*. The words of Achilles that he "would rather be a peasant in the sweet sunshine of earth than king of the Shades" points at the whole principle of it. But in *Enoch Arden* these peculiar coincidences are but a golden chain, only some of whose links however are visible, which from the first draws the hero to God because proving God's gracious care.

Prometheus' sufferings again (and let it be remarked that the contrast is not only allowable but full of meaning) prove to him nothing of this while he is enduring them; they are simply wrongs done to him by Destiny. And I must be pardoned if I take occasion to say here that those who suggest a reconciliation of Jove and his mangled victim by making the Deity the mere minister of beneficial discipline to the Titan for the spirit of the latter lost play of Æschylus defeat their own purpose. To do this would simply be to superimpose upon the classical form the soft uniting spirit of that which belongs solely to the more transcendent Christian mythus. At all events such an idea would to a very great extent brighten away the awful background of arbitrary fate, which first made it possible for the classical poets to bring out with such terrible distinctness, like vivid lightnings on clouds of blackness, the bolts of the anger of opposing gods. In the getting of this fulness of repose and spiritual roundedness, if one may speak so, the very form of the classical *epos* would disappear—would inevitably be swallowed up and lost. It is the shadow of a dark capricious Fate, dissociated from the idea of right and justice, which gives at once the inward grandeur of opposing attributes and the outward settledness and repose which characterize

one and all of these ancient dramas. It was an "igno-
miny of causeless wrong" Prometheus suffered, and
though he hopes for ultimate deliverance, that deliverance
is to come from a blind arbitrary fate identical with that
which has suffered him to be so lacerated for his heroic
effort on man's behalf. At any rate whatever theories
may be raised to reconcile the poem with itself, Prometheus in his suffering and while he suffers does not feel
in its fulness that

> Every cloud that spreads above,
> And veileth love, itself is love.

Nor whatever he may do afterwards does he while—

> Doomed to walk in company with pain
> And fear and bloodshed, miserable train,

in the Wordsworthian sense—

> Turn his necessity to glorious gain.

But Enoch, from the first and to the very end, and
that by no force of lofty, but transmitted character, as
in Prometheus, throughout all his sufferings, "reads
God's warning—wait," and in that patient waiting, and
not in any merely outward and capricious deliverance,
he completely vanquishes his unkind fate. It is in this
consideration that we see the grand use Tennyson
makes of Christianity; and hence he can never in the
mere form of his creation be rigid, lucid, and self-
composed, because he has not only to paint a simple,
sustained, and I might almost say, unprogressive mood
in his hero, but rather a mixed and complicated array

of moods, constantly, however, growing more and more harmonious. While, therefore, the aim of classical art was to make humanity subject to one overpowering mood for the sake of simplicity of outward form, just as the aim of all social arrangements seems to have been to develop one monotonous, though rudely healthy type of manhood; the aim of Christian art, as we all feel, is to break up rigid rules, and also dead material, and so to saturate all matter with a free, and withal joyous, because triumphant spirituality. Here, indeed, lies the one distinction between the classical and really Christian poem; and in no poem I know of are the elements— dark inscrutable caprices of Destiny—which played so large a part in classical poetry more freely used, and yet more completely conquered, and, so to speak, melted down by force of a higher faith than in *Enoch Arden*.

For if Enoch remembers these fateful, hateful shadows it is only ultimately to draw comfort from them, and triumph over mere fate by faith. He is no Stoic, bearing his misfortune with a passive and cold submission while the will is actually upborne by the irritating strain of the anguish which now alone relieves the monotony of existence. No; a nobler spirit is the impelling motive of his life. Now even, as when young, " he sets a purpose before his eyes," and his life is to the last an active one. He suffers truly: but then does he not also joy in his power of saving others from suffering, weak and poor as he is ?

If Annie drew a comfort in her worst hour by "setting her sad will to chime with Enoch's," Enoch now draws the deeper joy into his sorrowing,—even as the burnt sun-blasted earth draws more fully of the dew into its bosom—by "setting his sad will to chime with God's." The Stoics never dreamt of this form of the will's activity, and it has no place in the early dramas. And where the exercise of that will is shown so harmoniously to grow fuller, surer, grander towards the close I do not think it can be melancholy any more than it is to see a young bright spirit escaping from racking earthy sufferings into the full freedom which comes of faith and hope.

The Greek was haunted by the *shadow* of an Infinite from which, unlike us, he could by no possibility escape. To him Immortality had not been brought to *light*. His body might be free; but the Fate,—black, awful, ominous,—still followed on. Prometheus was relieved from his rock; not from the conditions of life which made the rock a possible punishment for him or his brethren. The Fate, in fact, was but the visual embodiment of those intellectual difficulties, in brooding over which lies the root of our own modern *sorrow*. But *Enoch Arden* is the beautiful assertion of an absolute freedom within the soul or will—the recognition and simple picturing out of a sphere which is all untouched of Time or Circumstance, and indeed cannot be intersected by these. Those questionings and querulous imaginings—futile attempts to wring out of the intellect an answer to the great problem of destiny—are put wholly aside. Duty, in one word, becomes the great solvent and saviour, and so it is that Enoch Arden dies, *rejoicing* that he has become a triumphant victor. In that innermost chamber of the being where alone true enjoyment and freedom tabernacle he possesses his purpose and is possessed of no desire, and thus he escapes from the toils of doubt, despair, and intellect out of which come mostly all human ills, pains, distresses.

The Prometheus waits it is true as does Enoch. But this because it has been revealed to him that a deliverer shall rescue him from his bodily torment; Enoch Arden waits with no promise save that of a blessed hereafter, and welcomes death more cheerfully than he did the sail which saved him from the loneliness of his island. If *Enoch Arden* is a "melancholy tale" then the melancholy has grown into what a quaint old English writer has called "the fine of sorrow" which "lies next to the heart of joy." But indeed in this one point we have the distinction between the two great worlds of art. It is a difference too, which as has been hinted enters into the form, and exhibits itself clearly there. The one is still, fixed, rigid, frigid, as it were bound and closed in at every point by form and rule—these the external images of that awful fate which haunted their half-darkened minds, as to a hereafter—the other all fluent, clear-flowing with one predominating earnest, yet calmly joyful mood which permeates the whole, and permits no portion to be viewed apart from its relation to the close and the reconciliation. And nowhere is that reconciliation more grandly and clearly shown than in *Enoch Arden*.

Enoch Arden is in fact the Promethean poem of the age, if the paradox will be allowed. There is, of course, a contradiction in calling a Christian mythus Promethean. But no single word could better express my meaning here. Each of the characters in Tennyson's poem is haunted by a fateful shadow of place or person, which with the Greek artists would have been an embodied fate, taking visual shape upon the stage. And yet how beautifully these are made to waver and disappear wholly at last. They exist; but simple Christian faith robs them of all power. Annie is haunted by a presentiment of Enoch's presence all the first year after her marriage with Philip; but when the new relation bodies itself forth in "an outward breathing type" with new duties and new claims, the faithful fulfilment of these drives away the awful shadow: it appears no more. A little piece of nature this, which is most skilfully used by Tennyson to give a fine and a true dramatic effect; and it is but one out of many illustrations of a like nature which might be cited in proof of the statements I have advanced. In the classical, nature or outer "circumstance," of which natural laws are but a portion, overpowers human will; which does not suffer shipwreck only because the body by careful ministration was constantly kept in the clearest health ; in the Christian again, of which *Enoch Arden* is our nineteenth century rhythmic statement, human will and human duty overpower and subdue all necessity and mere external force.

It is but a common-place to say that Providence always in a strange way interprets adverse circumstances if the subject of them is but willing to "read God's warning—wait." But if the poet is a *seer* at all, as I have always understood he is, his business is to prove by practical examples—by still, calm, picturesque ren-derings and through varied forms, that this truth is vital. To show the full meanings and relations of that which to other eyes is all isolated confusion, and as yet points not to harmony but to disorder (which of course means misery) is the business of those more highly-gifted than the mass of men ; and if this is done with clear aim and earnest desire the man is a poet though he may have written in prose. Bunyan's *Pilgrim* is one of the most perfect epics we have ; and I am not sure but out of the works of Jeremy Taylor or Sir Thomas Browne one might extract the material for an epic—lying in fact like gold in the earth. This then, however much it may be forgotten, is the real work or object of the poet, and more especially of the epic poet. But the very mention of such distinc-tions as that between lyric, epic and dramatic tends to confuse and mislead. As to the spirit there is no such distinction. To the poet *qua* poet it really does not exist. He is lyrical this moment, epical the next, and dramatic the one immediately after that. The form in which the poet will express himself will be very much determined by the point of outer circumstance he touches; for were he not to touch that he would never sing at all. In short the shape his thoughts about men will take will be according to the fashion of the day, or the sort of thing that will sell, or to please a patron, or to suit a theatrical audience, or perhaps to gratify the whim of a whimsical lover.

But, although William Shakspeare had been perfectly independent of the Globe Theatre, he would yet have written epical or lyrical dramas, simply because he saw more clearly into the secrets of mankind—had in himself more completely solved the difficult problems of human life than any other man; and because of his deeper sympathy and power over character he would have reflected his full-orbed soul through a thousand other creatures. Distinctions of an abstract arbitrary character, here as elsewhere, are never-ending. Is it not still matter of dispute whether this man was most poet or dramatist? And is it not the fact that in every article we read regarding him, surprise is expressed that in the then low state of the drama, and the artificial immoral fashions that prevailed, he should yet have told us so many everlasting truths? But that it was, the

very telling of these truths, which constituted Shakspeare a great poet; and he would have given expression
to these in whatever circumstances he had been placed,
only the form through which they would have shone
down upon us might have been very different indeed. So
that in point of fact these distinctions do not exist,
however necessary the recognition of them may be in
the sort of criticism now in vogue. Rather we might
say that the different species of poetry are related to
each other as bud, blossom, and fruit. Burns's *Mary
in Heaven* contains in it the germ of any epic the
ploughman could have written. Dante in a few verses
in the *Vita Nuova*, to which he most significantly refers
in the *Paradiso*, when he says :

> Questi fu tal nella sua Vita Nuova—
> (Such was he in the New Life,)

gives the key to his immortal poem, because in them
we have suggested to us the whole cause and principle
of his later spiritual development—his full faith in the
idea that Beatrice had turned towards him the whole
force of her purified being to lead him upward, and so
fulfil in a deeper spiritual bond that of which earthly
marriage is but a poor half-darkened symbol. And
through the epic there runs the echo of those earlier
lines, like a sweet subtle under-note relieving even the
awfulest pictures of the *Inferno*. And then a rather
popular writer who would perhaps quarrel with us here,
and yet with the *naïvest* remarks and hints cunningly

endeavour to re-establish the very distinction while seeming to agree with us, has, with an intuitive glance far beyond his half - Coleridgean critical philosophy, pointed out that the spirit of *In Memoriam* lies in the little lyric, "*Break, break, break,*" as the oak may be said to lie in the acorn. The lyrical in short is but the note on which a fuller musical harmony may be set.

But the one element in determining the question, Poet or not poet ? is whether he can introduce the " repose of reconcilement" for us. If so, he will "justify the ways of God to men " though he may not have intimated his set purpose of doing so. If a Christian singer misses this then he is only on the way to becoming a true poet—only sees confused portions of life as yet, the rainbow of beauty which shall span and give the promise of completeness to life not having risen on the cloud for him—till now he has only written bits, beginnings of poems, given us grand problems without even a hint at their solution. Homer himself was higher than such an one yet is ; because he had in his mind and had wrought out a complete scheme of life, though of course it never rose above a merely truthful natural level. Novalis, that strange literary witch, says that Goethe's greatness consisted in completing whatsoever he undertook. And Goethe himself gives the most direct illustration of the principle I am dealing with here. After the first part of the play of *Faust* had been published, and had been spoken of and written about a good deal, Goethe quietly wrought away at the second portion and took no notice of the criticisms, nor the attempts in the meantime made to continue it. But when he first published his second part he took occasion to express his surprise that it had not struck any one that the true and necessary continuation should carry the hero into a freer condition— elevated entirely away from the narrow, hampered, contradictory sphere of the first, so that the freedom and higher purpose attained by Faust should reconcile much that was, or seemed contradictory in the first portion. Goethe's remark shows how clearly he had fixed in his heart and brain the truth here illustrated. In fact the great German regarded the first part of *Faust* as the mere stating of a great problem which could only become truly poetical through the higher moral result attained in the life of the hero. Goethe, it is true, never outwardly completed his work because to have done so would have been to have followed his hero into a future state of existence ; and that lay not in Goethe's province. But the very fact of dramatic incompleteness in such a case has its moral corollary. Hamlet dies ; Faust dies ; but the individual will dies not, and in every true poem, epic or dramatic, we have a new and necessary assertion of the idea of a future existence, although the poet has no right to dogmatise, or to surround his picture with certain arbitrary promises as to the conditions of that future.

All this is seen in each of Shakspeare's dramas. How completely he reconciles all the discordant fearful elements of the play before he has done! It is indeed beautiful to see how with him vice is always punished; and that not because he set himself up as a moralist, but simply because he found it was true to fact. The universe, according to his reading of it, refused to second or sanction diabolism; and therefore by him too it is uniformly thrown out and defeated ultimately. And though the innocent are often engulfed in the conflagration that arises from the first fatal devil's spark it is a most peculiar circumstance that Shakspeare almost never uses the supernatural save for the purpose of showing on the one hand the victims in glory: and on the other the awful inward sufferings of the wrong-doers. Thus by the reading of any one of his plays we are confirmed in the thought that there is a Providence at the bottom of human affairs, which ultimately is and can only be on the side of right and virtue. And it is the same thing with Tennyson; he begins his story, tells it naturally, and with him as with Shakspeare, and for the same reason, virtue alone is permanently powerful, though in the laureate's case the influence is even more clear throughout with respect to the moral issues. The outer body of events is truthfully, naturally presented to us. We have invariably sorrow, disappointment and a hard struggle; but all is only a pathway to a grand result—to purify the spirit and show its victory.

And then though there has been much suffering, sorrow, crying and tears the poem quietly and grandly ends; and we feel that we have added to the sum of our human hopes and sympathies by reading it.

Let my readers just think for a moment of Philip Ray in *Enoch Arden.* "He has *his* dark hour unseen;" he doesn't revenge himself on Enoch: feels Enoch is the noblest strongest man among them; therefore gives place to him; enters into his own destiny—"embracing the purpose of God;" sticks closer to the mill and duty for satisfaction and escape from his own thoughts; wins a position, and because of it is able as he is willing to assist her he loves and hers when the cloud falls upon them so dense and dark. And then again Enoch—when he finds another in his stead, and "has *his* dark hour unseen," as he beholds joy and comfort circling the hearth from which he is excluded forevermore he does not avenge himself on Philip—nay blesses all of them with his last breath—even "the slighted suitor of old times;" for he feels Philip never wished him or his aught but good. It is a lyric of true love this *Enoch Arden* perpetually revolving upon itself and ever growing the completer to the eye the longer it is looked at.

The fact, too, that Tennyson's hero is by Providence so fixed for long years to bear in awful solitude the stings of his own sad thoughts with no relief from the overwhelming contrasts and suggestions that memory must perpetually throw forth upon him, would go still

further to justify the parallel I have instituted between
Enoch Arden and the *Prometheus*. But notice one
essential difference in which is formally drawn, if I may
put it so, a confirmation of this idea. The *Prometheus*
is a cold, rigid, statuesque figure bound to a bare
ragged Caucasian rock, which for the purposes of art
would form a complete picture in itself; and was in
its awful stillness kept almost throughout the whole
play before the eyes of the spectators. But in Enoch
Arden's island we have the rich variety, the many-
colouredness of the modern life and spirit; and this
seeming-freedom or variety of external elements, by the
cunning of art is only made to intensify the sufferings
of the hero by deepening his gloom, which yet he
completely vanquishes. And then Enoch's isle is
distant, suggested, brought before us more in idea,
by intense sympathetic attraction of mood. Even when
we are directly pointed to the island in its eastern glory,
we lose it again in the broad, glowing zone of sea, the
rich deep sky, the large luminous near-seeming stars,
which all at first only go to sharpen the pangs of poor
Enoch. It may be said however in answer to this—the
one is a drama and the other a lyrico-epic poem and
you make too much of the contrast you have instituted.
Perhaps there is from one point of view a ray of truth
in this. But as I have said already we have in those
days gone to very extreme lengths in these superfine
formal distinctions which do not exist for the poet, and

only live in the intellect of the critic. I have always felt that the spirit of poetry was very much like that spirit in the legend who got into all men's bodies and looked at things through their eyes.

From Sophocles and Æschylus to Tennyson what a stretch and also what a development! For in the Greek drama we see man under the iron thrall of circumstance and conquered by it. Faith, if he have a faith, is but the reflex of a sad despair, which made him enjoy this life, though full of shadows, only because the next life itself was but one great all-encircling shadow. In the drama of Shakspeare—best typified in *Hamlet*—man plays out his game with "circumstance"—and in the fact of his joying in the very power of freely facing these startling and awful problems of human destiny we see the transition from fate to faith. Hamlet because he is so convinced that there is a power of human will that could baffle and overcome all "circumstance" solves the enigma for humanity, though he but half-solves it for himself. Because of his peculiar psychological conformation it is not given to him to overcome; but he believes this *is* possible to man, and because he is so firm in this faith he accepts the fearful task presented to him, and engages in it only however to waste his powers and at last dash out his life. For what a short-sighted idea that is which would limit the meaning of *Hamlet* to a mere historical interpretation of certain old conventional notions of filial revenge. That old idea is but the body through

which an eternal truth of human nature speaks. Hamlet
with all his toils and troubles but types a stage through
which we must all pass. When the great Sphinx-problem
of duty is presented to us it is with us as with Hamlet—
we *must* solve it or be torn in pieces. I say Hamlet
prevailed inasmuch as there are some defeats which are
victories. In his will he conquered; but his will was
prisoned in a too-sensitive organism and it broke down
under the frightful strain. Inherited physical weakness or
morbid self-introspection is one form of "circumstance."
This was the little flower-vase in which according to
Goethe the tree of Hamlet's will was planted and which
was so sadly shattered and broken. It is much the same
problem that is throughout dealt with in the Shakspearean
drama. Hamlet more broadly viewed is the first statement evidently and Shakspeare consonantly with the
idea in the last verse of *Maud* where the near or the
domestic relations are practically placed first, makes his
first purely a domestic drama,—a drama of family affection. The solution is not given historically; for indeed
it cannot be so given wholly. Man so long as he is in
Time is imprisoned in it and is so far the slave of his
environment; but Hamlet essentially subdues his fate
in so meeting it. But in the Tennysonian drama (for
Maud is in spirit a lyrical-drama) we have the full
clear expression of the Christian idea. The subtle forces
of Christianity work visibly through the hero's life.
We see them in their results just as we may know where

sweet rivulets run underground by the richness of the grasses and herbs all along the irregular track. And at last it does well forth into clear day, giving at the end a tone of triumphant repose and peaceful reconcilement. All along we see it—during morbid isolation, love, despair, madness itself, and out it comes at length in full calm diapason of faith.

Many readers doubtless might be inclined to censure me for not having quoted some of those exquisite pieces of description such as that of Enoch's eastern isle. But what most attracts us in all these passages is the wonderful play of human affection, which actually interpenetrates dead matter and makes it the living symbol of thought and feeling. Tennyson never describes for the mere sake of producing a piece of fine or powerful description as Byron or Thomson would do; he always closely identifies himself with the scene so that it is transfigured by force of character or soul. The life that pulses through the universe is not a dim pantheistic something that he can lightly and carelessly sport with— not what Coleridge would have called the *ordo ordinans;* but a warm personality with which the higher impulses and aspirations of that great human heart of his are in perfect accord—the heart rejoicing ever to find itself so deeply in harmony with the soul of things. It is the poet's mood that has the beauty in it so that it can enkindle and glorify whatsoever it touches that belongs to earth. Thus the purely descriptive portions of these poems are highly moral and richly symbolic. His picture or rather series of pictures in the *Palace of Art* is by no means an arbitrary or wildly unmeaning association of objects, but is intensely significant and expresses the essential character of his genius—the power of cunningly translating common objects into symbols of the highest spiritual truths.

This point is worthy of a little attention. In the " Palace of Art " we have what seems an almost incongruous arrangement of beautiful forms. A deeper study reveals to us that they are carefully outlined pictures of deep human experiences. Every line, so distinct and clear as really to approach to the simplest prose, stands for an individual fact of life. By a sweet gradually-ascending scale, you have the soul's history definitely marked. The first picture is youth—flushed, hurried, active and never wearied—

> For some (rooms) were hung with arras green and blue,
>   Showing a gaudy summer morn,
> Where with puff'd cheek the belted hunter blew
>   His wreathed bugle-horn.

But across the mind even in the midst of this youthful haste and free physical outflowing come streaks of shadow—blights of doubt. For,

> One seem'd all dark and red—a track of sand,
>   And some one pacing there *alone*,
> Who paced for ever in a glimmering land,
>   Lit with a low large moon.

Dashing waves and winds even visit him with threats of buffeting.

> One show'd an iron coast and angry waves.
>   You seemed to hear them climb and fall
> And roar rock-thwarted under bellowing caves
>   Beneath the windy wall.

And even painful horrors come :—

> And one, a full-fed river, winding slow
>   By herds upon an endless plain,
> The ragged rims of thunder brooding low,
>   With shadow-streaks of rain.

But then once more come relapse and repose for a moment in the enjoyment of homely delights and pleasures and toils.

> And one, the reapers at their sultry toil.
>   In front they bound the sheaves.   Behind
> Were realms of upland, prodigal in oil,
>   And hoary to the wind.
> And one, an English home—gray twilight poured
>   On dewy pastures, dewy trees,
> Softer than sleep—all things in order stored,
>   A haunt of ancient peace.

Then through the region of art and legend he passes on till he is lost in the classic with its deadness of lines and cold rigid exactness of delineation; and here he hopes to find rest and peace in the worship of beautiful forms : hence he says :—

> Or sweet Europa's mantle blew unclasp'd,
>   From off her shoulder backward borne :
> From one hand drooped a crocus ; one hand grasped
>   The mild bull's golden horn.

> Or else flushed Ganymede, his rosy thigh
>   Half buried in the eagle's down,
> Sole as a flying star shot thro' the sky
>   Above the pillar'd town.

The rest of the poem describes the reaction from this sort of worship through misanthropy, isolation and misery to the true idea of art and life in the realizing of common duty and the filling up faithfully of the lowliest relations of every day. The picture is so complete and full of meaning that one is astonished so many men of keen critical faculty should have dealt with the poem and yet missed it. The description of Enoch Arden on his solitary island also very aptly illustrates and proves the truth of the above remark :—

> The mountain wooded to the peak, the lawns
> And winding glades high up like ways to heaven,
> The slender coco's drooping crown of plumes,
> The lightning flash of insect and of bird,
> The lustre of the long convolvuluses
> That coil'd around the stately stems, and ran
> Ev'n to the limit of the land, the glows
> And glories of the broad belt of the world,
> All these he saw ; but what he fain had seen
> He could not see, the kindly human face, .
> Nor ever hear a kindly voice, but heard
> The myriad shriek of wheeling ocean fowl,
> The league-long roller thundering on the reef,
> The moving whisper of huge trees that branch'd
> And blossomed in the zenith, or the sweep
> Of some precipitous rivulet to the wave,
> As down the shore he ranged, or all day long
> Sat often in the seaward-gazing gorge,
> A shipwreck'd sailor, waiting for a sail ;

No sail from day to day, but every day
The sunrise broken into scarlet shafts
Among the palms and ferns and precipices ;
The blaze upon the waters to the east ;
The blaze upon his island overhead ;
The blaze upon the waters to the west ;
Then the great stars that globed themselves in heaven,
The hollower-bellowing ocean, and again
The scarlet shafts of sunrise—but no sail.

There often as he watch'd, or seem'd to watch,
So still, the golden lizard on him paused,
A phantom made of many phantoms moved
Before him haunting him, or he himself
Moved haunting people, things and places, known
Far in a darker isle beyond the line ;
The babes, their babble, Annie, the small house,
The climbing street, the mill, the leafy lanes,
The peacock-yewtree and the lonely Hall,
The horse he drove, the boat he sold, the chill
November dawns and dewy-glooming downs,
The gentle shower, the smell of dying leaves,
And the low moan of leaden-colour'd seas.

Once likewise, in the ringing of his ears,
Tho' faintly, merrily—far and far away—
He heard the pealing of his parish bells ;
Then, tho' he knew not wherefore, started up
Shuddering, and when the beauteous hateful isle
Return'd upon him, had not his poor heart
Spoken with That, which being everywhere
Lets none, who speaks with Him, seem all alone,
Surely the man had died of solitude.

It will be noticed here how beautifully affection plays
throughout. The one is a " beautiful hateful isle ; "
the other is a " darker isle beyond the line ; " but human

affection has transfigured this last, and made it loveliest to Enoch.

Aylmer's Field seems to me defective as a whole in which respect most of Tennyson's other poems are such marvellous successes. Nor do I detect any deeper currents of thought and purpose as in *The Princess.* It is simply a love-story made up of such elements as in my humble opinion would have been best treated in prose. But perhaps a new world may suddenly strike out of it some day, as the beholder "stands silent on a peak in Darien." This has frequently happened to admirers of Tennyson with his poems, and they are constantly discovering fresh beauties and new meanings even in the oldest ones. That is a conclusive proof of their genuinely poetical nature. " Are not all truly beautiful faces ugly at the first, then?" said a thoughtful lady once. So it may be asked are not all true poems quiet and almost commonplace at first? They should not discover all their meaning and worth at once. Perhaps it may be so with *Aylmer's Field.* We have here some beautiful individual passages and some full-toned denunciations which are skilfully set to verse. But a critic would only act wisely in not committing himself by being too definite, as it *might* chance that the laureate has touched up an old piece long laid aside to make sport of our poor fraternity in a gentle way by actually emptying his waste basket on their devoted heads.

As a piece of genuine dramatic idealistic-realism *The Grandmother* is perhaps as perfect a specimen as we have! How true to life! What quaint turns of expression! What a well of garrulous *naïveté !* and all so subtly run together, so fused as one might say into a consistent compacted whole. This piece indeed belongs to the highest region of poetry; and one might ask what does its beauty arise from but simply the intense sympathy that pervades it and its near approach in form to ordinary language?

The only other notable poems in this volume are *Tithonus* and the *Northern Farmer*. The former is a fine rendering of a classical legend, and proceeding on the idea formerly expressed that Tennyson would never now play with an old form unless it had some reference to a modern truth we try to extract something for the present time from it. Well, as Tithonus asked the goddess Aurora for immortality but forgot to ask youth and wandered aged and miserable, so we in this age have prayed fervently for material progress—for temporal wealth; and have got our prayer answered, have annihilated, as we say, one form of space and time by railway and another by telegraph, have subdued the earth and glorified ourselves in our merely marketable commodities. But we find no rest for our souls in these, because we have forgotten the avenging laws of nature in the evanescent delight of our answered request; and are always praying for something more. We pant to regain a fuller, clearer, closer relation to the infinite, the invisible; and in our half-drunk, half-fevered, full-bellied stupor fancy we will perhaps get a ray of it in Davenport *séances*, mesmeric experiments, clairvoyance, table-rapping, &c. But we will not get it that way. "The gods themselves cannot recall their gifts," neither can our God recall the past and its results on human character. And so we must plod on artificial, grey-haired because grey-souled—bent down before our time and actually overcome of material saturation and *ennui*. Then we run from this extreme to that and sometimes sink down exhausted in our *ennui*. The word recalls to mind a passage from the prose poet of our day—"You may mount on our railways and ride at the rate of fifty or if you please five hundred miles an hour—you may stalk deer on the rings of Saturn or do yacht-voyaging under the belts of Jupiter, but that all-encircling *ennui* will still surround you. You cannot escape from it, you can but change your place in it without solacement. With all these mountains of material implements such as men never had before you are yet unable to do any great fruitful work; but I say be thankful for your *ennui* it is your last mark of manhood." I fancy one can find all that in Tennyson's *Tithonus*. The pathos of the line—"If I be he that watched"—is inimitable, expressing very fitly our relation to that grandly old simple life which we yet watch and half-reverence, but have no power in ourselves to revive. That this poem

will bear some such interpretation as this I feel convinced.   Here are a few powerful lines :—

> Alas ! for this gray shadow, once a man—
> So glorious in his beauty and thy choice,
> Who madest him thy chosen, that he seem'd
> To his great heart none other than a God !
> I ask'd thee, " Give me immortality."
> Then didst thou grant mine asking with a smile,
> Like wealthy men who care not how they give.
> But thy strong Hours indignant work'd their wills,
> And beat me down and marr'd and wasted me,
> And tho' they could not end me, left me maim'd
> To dwell in presence of immortal youth,
> Immortal age beside immortal youth,
> And all I was, in ashes.
> . . . . Let me go : take back thy gift :
> Why should a man desire in any way
> To vary from the kindly race of men,
> Or pass beyond the goal of ordinance
> Where all should pause, as is most meet for all ?

Tithonus, stupid fellow, might have discovered, had
he only thought, that in the granting of his wish a law
was violated which would inevitably avenge itself upon
him slowly and sorely.   Had he but honestly reflected
for a little he would have seen that all his enjoyment
while under the empty delusion was in direct opposition
to nature ; and that, simply because he had consciously
made himself an exception to the wide human experience.
There is no happiness apart from our fellow men : the
deepest misery of a lone-stricken soul is to be cast out
from them and to have no part or lot in their lowly
interests.   We sigh for inspirations ; what we need is

humility. We wish, each one, to have a sphere apart ; and forget that if the world was not made for one but for all, neither was Immortality brought to light for units. And so it is that we realize now as in past times that " the gods do plague men by granting them their wishes." In our artificial ways, in our every-day violations of nature and of fact, in our greed, our isolation, and our separating selfishness can we not see that some reference is made to *us* here ? Tithonus' fate is a warning to us—a warning veiled it is true : but only veiled as the mystic figure of Sais was veiled—to express the more powerfully the half-hidden truth to those who have eyes to see. Tennyson in this poem directly joins issue with Carlyle, Ruskin and the rest who day by day are loudly calling us back to simplicity and kindliness, and to harmony with those delibe-rately avenging laws on which the world itself is built.

Poor Tithonus, aged and tortured in his body, was indeed a "gray shadow, once a man : " but with what force does the picture come home to us of this age in this way of reading it, who have buried our souls in bales of merchandise—in flesh, and so go wandering restless and *aged in soul.* That idea indeed gives the poem an infinitely powerful moral, and application to our time—the " strong Hours indignant," now as then working their wills upon poor, selfish, proud and ambi-tious men.

I am very well aware it may here be objected that

by such an interpretation of this poetical gem I have in some measure taken away from it the broad, innate, universal beauty and significance—the generic meaning for each individual in every age—the warning for one and all of us to see that in our askings we ask not amiss, and suffer; and I am also aware that it might be advanced regarding this view of mine that it tends just rather much to impute a definite self-consciousness to the poet in his work.   But then I would reply to this that the poet always reaches through the universal to the particular, through the abstract and general to the individual and concrete, in order that he may wed the particular with the general again; and so unite in one breathing bond of life the past and the present, the old and the new. /The poet cannot escape from his own time, nor can he live apart from it even though he would. /Of a truth his conceptions should flow from him with as much freedom and with as noble an unconsciousness as though the form they took was pure and noble deed.   But then the singer and the doer as well must discern clearly the claims of the moment, the great requirements of the day, so that the one may decisively do his work and the other directly utter his message fitly and to purpose.   The one must speak in the language and idiom of the time so that men may understand, and he must also speak out of deep sympathy with their habits and ways of thought so that his message may be at once *believed* and reverenced;

while the other must readily and unselfishly do what all
men will acknowledge it was noble to do and fruitful
and blessed in the doing. Absolutely without self-
consciousness there is no man and no poet. But let us
thank the Divine Beneficences that on the other hand
there is hardly a man who does not keep hold of some
virtues of which he is quite unconscious and that there
is no true poet who is not far richer in vital influences
for good than he himself ever dreamed. Glancing over
one of Mr. Ruskin's books the other day I came upon
a passage which may be set down here as throwing some
welcome light on this point. He writes:—" I believe
the true mind of a nation, at any period, is always best
ascertainable by examining that of its greatest men. . .
It is a constant law that the greatest men, whether
poets or historians, live entirely in their own age, and
that the greatest fruits of their work are gathered out of
their own age. . . The work of these great idealists
is always universal, not because it is *not portrait* but
because it is *complete* portrait down to the heart, which
is essentially the same in all ages. Thus Tintoret and
Shakspeare paint, both of them, simply Venetian and
English nature as they saw it in their time, down to the
root ; and it does for *all* time ; but as for any care to
cast themselves into the particular ways and tones of
thought or custom of past time in their historical work
you will find it in neither of them, nor in any other
perfectly great man that I know of." As I recognize

the deep truth in these sentences I am inclined rather to claim for Tennyson the particular merit in this *Tithonus* of painting, though indirectly and half-unconsciously, his own time and its besetting curse, than to belaud him for the utterance of generic truths which after all would only have relation to the age in the very measure that the age found itself specially reflected therein.

Were I to venture on a comparison of Keats and Tennyson as interpreters of old classical forms, I would be led to express myself somewhat in this way. Keats followed the beautiful as allying itself with external form mainly, and this to the neglect of the true appertaining to the essential spirit which almost unconsciously even to the classical artists themselves expressed fixed and eternal laws. Keats in short worshipped Beauty in preference to Truth. Tennyson again always finds the essential truths, and indeed, never uses an old form or image without all along holding by the human spirit it contains; and his purpose is once more to connect that with the flowing current of life, and directly show its relation to the present. Keats, in short, merged or buried the present and its claims in cold dead lines of materialism and was actually more a heathen in his worship of these Greek gods than were the Greeks themselves. Tennyson on the other hand has so mastered the old culture that he can use it, like a true Christian man, as a spectacle through which to read all times and the different outer developments of human nature. This idea as to Keats' position in regard to the old Greek mythology is not original. Wordsworth seized it; and I daresay grieved that no ray of higher Christian light had so penetrated the soul of Keats as to enable him to do, as some one has said Shakspeare accomplished in such a degree—"put all his old Greeks and Romans to a Christian school, and thus made them higher beings and true to nature, while yet the forms, feelings, circumstances special to the time, are preserved for us." When after having heard Keats read his *Hymn to Pan* no other remark could be got out of Wordsworth but that it was a "pretty piece of Paganism," Keats and his inconsiderate friends might have reflected; for Wordsworth spoke simple truth. And there is a serious consideration proper here. No man has a right to toy, and waste his God-given time and gifts in the manner Keats did, with the decoration of dead ideas in fanciful and playful resurrection. Such ideas deserve to die when the truth of them could either be no longer seen or believed, which truth was these old nations' reading of the laws of the universe. We should be too busy and too earnest to enjoy such a thing;—and therefore one can hardly prophesy for Keats the immortality he so much hungered after. In truth immortality comes most readily to those who hold by practical work and let their ideas take care of themselves. We can hardly conceive that our Bible is all the literature of the

Jewish nation from first to last, or that it is even what idle fanciful people in old days often thought the highest; but it is all that has come down to us; and, apart from theories of inspiration, we have there the record of the most earnest struggling lives in all Judea from its first formation till its end—biographies more or less imperfect—as all biographies are—of those who were purest and lived most in harmony with the spirit of freedom and faith. Job, David, Samuel,—all these are poets because of what they lived and did; and the ultimate test, as it is the source of all true poetry, is noble living. Only "the pure in heart see God;" there is not much seen truly that is not seen through Him directly or indirectly, and do we not call the poet a *Seer?*

The Northern Farmer is likewise a most wonderful poem—perhaps the most so in one point of view Tennyson has yet written. There are so many elements in it and here there is proof of the existence of a faculty for broad humour which the poet has never before exercised—*Will Waterproof's Monologue* being of a quite different and lighter cast. But here you have such glances into character, recorded too with a single touch as if with the graver of a Retzsch! Tennyson's muse in this poem becomes grandly and severely dramatic. The first broad feature we detect in the character of the *Northern Farmer* is his truth to nature—his harmony with lower natural forces. His knowledge is certainly not wide; indeed he scarcely knows anything beyond his farming; but then he has a joy in good farming one would almost say apart from the idea that it pays best. But if our farmer doesn't know a great deal he is far more true to what he does know than most cultured men are. For his unswerving obedience to nature ; joy in his work simply for its own sake ; and for his faithfulness to moral requirements so long as these are carefully kept separate from the abstract sphere,—for all this he ought to be admired and honoured of Mr. Carlyle. For he is true to himself and his own nature, and never has, or could have run his head against the wall of fact by fancies and empty theories. Though, like all men of narrow knowledge, he is exclusive with regard to ideas, yet practically he is most tolerant of men themselves—can bear with them as he does with nature herself—her storms, her hail and her horrid weeds that will spring up in his way and in his fields. He cannot believe in abstract truth because in fact his mind is not formed to understand it. His sense however is keen and it has enabled him to read a thing or two in nature, in change of season, needs of the earth, &c., and to wisely apply these lessons. He tries to do his duty to each one; for he has most earnestly set up before himself a standard of duty. But he has begun to build on the very lowest platform one would say ; and his life verifies a remark I have seen somewhere that if one is only true to the lower side of truth it will rise up with him and turn its upper side to him. For having come to the idea that "the lond," or the mere clods (about the last thing a cultured man would find soul in) has claims upon him—that in fact he has a *duty* to do to it as to a human being, the result is that as he stolidly, steadily acts up to his idea " the lond " rises upwards one would say, whilst men it would actually seem have to come down a little to meet it.   For our farmer refuses to square off his practice by any other standard than this of " the lond."   None other indeed exists for him.   But then low as his standard is he keeps on the whole true to it.   Custom is one powerful form of law to him, and he unintelligibly worships it as he does a hundred other things.   All abstract talk against his habits is nonsense to him, and therefore in direct contradiction to the doctor's advice and even to his own danger he will have his usual allowance of " Yaüle."   His is a nature, which at first view would seem impenetrable by any of what are called the finer sentiments or feelings, and yet he prizes dearly the respectful regards of men—puts a value on their opinions of him and of his doings.   He says :—

> Looäk 'ow quoloty smoiles when they sees ma a passin' by
> Says to thessën naw doot what a mon a beä sewer-ly.

And observe the weight of the reason that he feels certain justifies their so doing.   Though "squoire's in Lunnon " he is no eye-servant and never has been, and they all know that too—

> They knaws what I beän to squoire sin' fust a' comed to the 'All,
> I done my duty by squoire an' I done my duty by all.

He has no power of self-examination such as the parson speaks vaguely about on Sundays—no power even of metaphysical introspection : he sees himself only in one thing and that is work firmly doggedly done, and that too not so much for his own sake as for " squoire's." Nor can his stolid mind harbour even a relic of the superstitious. He certainly admits the existence of ghosts in words; but he has never seen one, and in the particular case before him he knows that the popular idea was most mistaken. The turn of the first line is exquisitely truthful and humorous as expressive of a mind which has an intense delight in ranging over old plans and changes :—

D'ya moind the waäste, my lass? naw, naw, tha was na born
   then,
Theer wur a boggle in it; I often heerd un mysen ;
Moäst loike a butter-bump (bittern) for I heerd un aboot an-
   aboot ;
But I stubbed un oop wi' the lot an' raved an' rembled un oot.

And what a satire we have here upon those weakly in-tellectual, very orthodox parsons, of whose sermons more than the *Northern Farmer* could truthfully say :—

I 'eerd un a bummin' awaäy like a buzzard-clock * ower my yeäd,
An' I niver knaw'd what a' meaned ; but I thowt a 'ad summat
   to saäy,
An' I thowt a' said whot a owt to a said an' I comed awaäy.

The serious bedside talk of such an one as parson is mixed

---

* Cockchafer.

up with "toithes"—is "easy an' freeä," and the reflection
is forced upon the strong stolid man :—

I weänt saäy men be loiars thof summun said it in aäste
But a reiids wonn sarmin a weeäk an' I a' stubbed Thornaby
    waäste.

The two last stanzas of the poem are inimitable. As
expressive of the honest feelings of a large class of old
country people, now almost extinct, who seemed to have
no possible point of contact with new ideas and could
only relate themselves to them by excluding them, it is
unequalled.   Nothing could be better than the following
from a man in what threatens to be his last illness,
and who still has on his mind "the lond" that has
fed, and clad him and been his chief joy :—

But summun 'ull come ater meä mayhap wi' is kittle o' steäm
Huzzin' an maäzin' the blessed feälds wi' the Divil's oän team.
Gin I mun doy I mun doy, an' loife they says is sweet,
But gin I mun doy I mun doy, for I couldn abear to see it.

This feeling however is not specially English.   I
have met with it often among the old people in Scotland.   In the end of 1864 an old woman in Caithness-
shire was met on the road by a neighbour who asked
whether she was going to see the steam-plough Lord
Caithness was working on one of his farms, and which
was of course attracting a great deal of attention in the
north.   But the old woman's reply given with the
utmost seriousness and gravity of countenance was—
" Lord ! keep my sight and eyes from viewing vanity."

In the last verse there is also a fine glimpse of truth. Often has the writer seen old people of both sexes in Scotch farmhouses attract the servants away from their work by gossip about old things—maundering recollections; and then on a moment's interval take occasion to " flite " or scold at the waste of time. And so our farmer :—

What atta stannin' theer for, an' doesn bring ma the yaüle,
Doctor's a 'tottler, lass, an a's hallus i' the owd taäle ;
I weänt breük rules for Doctor, a knaws naw moor nor a floy ;
Git ma my yaäle I tell tha, an' gin I mun doy I mun doy.

He is a strange mixture of rudeness, sincerity, sensitiveness, honesty, belief, disbelief, and a hundred other contradictory things. But he is true to what he professes—faithful to what he does see of the truth. The picture is not without its meaning for us who are so taken up with empty fancies, theories and ideas. Assuredly we may learn a lesson from one who so excludes all such, and like a blunt Saxon man holds intently to his daily work, feeling and firmly believing that the doing of that well is the fulfilling of a great duty.

There is just one other short remark I desire to make before closing. It is with regard to the pure Saxon words which Tennyson invariably uses in preference to other and more modern words. It has been well said that " if the Anglo-Saxon genius vanished under the influence of the Conquest, it was as a river which sinks into and runs under the soil, and which will issue forth

again after the lapse of hundreds of years." Tennyson
is a real Saxon man, yearning for the practical, the
concrete, but by necessity in contact with conflicting
moods, because born in a time of hurry and speculation.
But though he paints all these moods faithfully he yet
points his reader uniformly beyond them, and hence as
I have shown the ends of his poems are naturally
enough the most significant and precious. This Tennyson is indeed a near relative of our earliest singers—
a star that in later times has burst forth beside our
constellation of " early morning-stars of song " and of
kindred with them. Though he bears with him all the
thought, and enters, in a most manly spirit, into all the
complicated culture and varied, confused, contradictory
moods of the present, yet his instruments are of the
simplest, identical with those our old, old fathers wrought
with. The richness, the wealth, the many-coloured-
ness of modern culture may give a complexness and by
consequence an occasional obscurity to his mood ; but
his words in themselves are never obscure—rather clear
and simple, like the eye of some gentle girl in whose
azure depths great thoughts and feelings lie hidden,
yet open and confessed. Several illustrations of this
suggest themselves to me. A little poem titled *The
Sailor Boy* will serve my object here as well as any.
Its purpose is to show how in the voyage of life after
even the grosser temptations have been vanquished, the
affections of race and family—so good in themselves—

may yet come in distracting the mind in its dutiful work. But here as will be noticed the spirit of the youth is victorious over all forms of temptation. Reading this little lyric one cannot help picturing those strange early adventurers, to whom we owe so much, on their rude skiffs or rafts turning a last long look back at the homes and the tender ones they are leaving behind ; and then dashing aside the thought and urging on their craft the more powerfully that new far-outstretching worlds awaited them in the distance. The painting in this little poem is wonderfully fresh and clear—a soft morning effect runs through it one might say—the words are of the simplest Saxon and the meaning of the very fullest and deepest :—

> He rose at dawn, and, fired with hope,
>   Shot o'er the seething harbour-bar,
> And reached the ship and caught the rope,
>   And whistled to the morning star.
>
> And while on deck he whistled loud,
>   He heard a fierce mermaiden cry,
> " Boy, though thou art young and proud,
>   I see the place where thou wilt lie.
>
> " The sands and yeasty surges mix
>   In caves about the dreary bay,
> And on thy ribs the limpet sticks,
>   And in thy heart the scrawl shall play ! "
>
> " Fool," he answered, " death is sure
>   To those that stay and those that roam ;
> But I will never more endure
>   To sit with empty hands at home.

" My mother clings about my neck,
  My sisters clamour, ' Stay, for shame ! '
My father raves of death and wreck,
  They are all to blame—they are all to blame.

" God help me ! save I take my part
  Of danger on the roaring sea,
A devil rises in my heart
  Far worse than any death to me."

And so with this little spirited Saxon song we take leave of the subject for the present, expressing our satisfaction that our poet is still simply Alfred Tennyson —a name embalmed and cherished, not only for what it symbolizes of thought and great work done for England, Englishmen and the world; but also because it tells of what has been wisely repented of, put under foot, or better still departed from and left wholly undone. For now-a-days as in the long ago the greatest teaching is that which is sacred and unconscious, which is deep and inexpressible in words, and because Tennyson has taught us silently so much I have placed him thus in close juxtaposition with the giant—Thomas Carlyle.

JOHN RUSKIN,

ART-CRITIC AND MORALIST.

OF all the distinguished writers of the present day, there is none who seems, at first sight, so diffuse and digressive as Ruskin. To the ordinary reader, his books are a sort of surprise and medley, from which he turns with a vague pleasure—it may be with the consciousness of moral feeling strengthened and confirmed, but without that full satisfaction and sense of benefit which might be felt after the study of a far less powerful writer. But the reason, after all, is obvious enough to those who have made closer acquaintance with Ruskin. He carries along with him many elements and tendencies which would need to be separated and seen apart before the great majority could form anything like a correct estimate of his character and ways of thought. Sometimes simple and clear as a child, he beguiles us by his unaffected and artless love of nature, discovering many beauties in what we had before passed over as trivial and commonplace; then again he is so subtle, farthoughted, and occasionally paradoxical, throwing out so much of a strange and novel character, that we are actually confused amid the hurry and potency of his thoughts : and then sometimes he presents the most gorgeous and impressive pictures with all the attraction of skilful contrast, drawing us back to him with the trust and confidence we always feel towards the true poet or artist. And so suddenly does he ring the changes that all these characteristics are frequently to be met with in one single short chapter. Considering these things, it can hardly surprise us that he is not, in the ordinary sense, *popular*, for, to be popular, requires one decided and striking element of character rather than many in peculiar and perplexing union. The very richness of a nature is sometimes inimical to its immediate effect upon the mass, just as the sparkling brilliancy of the player's over-jewelled hand may tend to disturb the hearing of sweet simple music.

But there is nevertheless one decided element of popularity in Ruskin. This is his remarkable and ready power of giving sensuous form to all his impressions, whether they be graver or gayer, simpler or more complex, staid or wayward, generic or more peculiar to himself. With him it would seem that to feel is to embody ; his experiences be they commoner or deeper, almost of themselves start into beautiful and appropriate form, in which we see the results of large culture and well-directed imagination. Ancient writers and recent ones alike serve him; he scruples not to borrow an old idea or expression, when it suits his purpose, usually also improving what he borrows; and around his every sentence there breathes the spirit of true manhood and genuine poetry. In this respect he might well claim to rank among our imaginative-descriptive poets, and would most assuredly take precedence of some of the more recent of them. Little lyrics—lyrics in all but the external niceties of form, on which some people lay so much stress in these days—will be found nestling in the corners of his chapters; the spirit of a true idyl lies occasionally in the cunning turn of a phrase; and the actual text for a sort of prose-epic he often finds in the figure in a fresco, or the wind-worn lines on a Venetian shaft.

And he is so sincere, reverent and tender withal. Into all the varied subjects he treats he carries one spirit and that is eminently a religious one in the truly human sense of it. His is a tremblingly sensitive nature as of a woman, with perceptions so keen as sometimes even to seem morbidly acute. Almost all he touches becomes suffused with the colouring derivable alone from a devoutness of spirit, which consecrates and beautifies much that is usually neglected or despised. And this innate fineness of nature is most harmoniously combined with other and bolder elements. We never miss token of a manly decisiveness, a healthy ardour, and a breadth and firmness of grasp. Thus we have a character at once peculiarly delicate, and peculiarly strong, the delicacy being of such a kind as to softly and expressively wed itself with those loftier if sterner attributes of courage, will and unwearied application.

But the popular element in Ruskin, to which I have referred, was unfortunately to some extent hidden by the form in which his earlier books appeared and the special purpose with which he originally set out. Appearing at first merely as an art-critic, and besides, narrowing his sphere to the interpretation of the works of an individual artist, it is matter of wonder more than anything else that his first book should have asserted for itself the place it has done among our English classics. This circumstance of itself augurs great force of mind and originality of character on his part, and on the part of the public a discrimination and appreciation of true excellence for which there is a decided tendency to give it but little credit. I must here confess, however, that I scarcely know whether to regard it as a fortunate circumstance or a misfortune that Mr. Ruskin at the outset was led in this outward and nominal way to narrow the range of his influence. Beyond question the consequence of his doing so was to hinder somewhat the full recognition of his greatness in that broader sphere he was at once destined and well fitted to fill— the sphere, I mean, of the moral and spiritual teacher. The influence upon Mr. Ruskin himself of the many misunderstandings and misinterpretations of the *Modern Painters*, I do not doubt for an instant has been a beneficial one. Endowed by nature with rare gifts, he had also been blessed by Providence with ample means. He had thus enjoyed fullest leisure to reflect and to perfect his thoughts about art and nature without the necessity of compromising himself or filtering away his faculties by journalism in any form of it. He had travelled a great deal, indeed one may say, had exhausted the art-treasures and museums of the Continent as well as those in England. His opinions and impressions on every point had been carefully tested and re-tested. The natural result was a settled and perfect confidence in the strength of his position, which somehow tended to produce in him an air of intolerance, sometimes amounting even to fretful impatience of contradiction. The skirmish which took place over *Modern Painters* taught him first of all this great practical lesson, that argument is of little worth in any department of inquiry, and especially so in the more purely spiritual one; and that the man who is convinced of the goodness of his position best proves it by being guardedly calm and imperturbably patient and self-contained. For Mr. Ruskin the circumstance of his first writing under such apparent narrowing conditions could be no permanent disadvantage, as indeed such never is, nor can be, to the truly noble and gifted. But to the public it was in one respect a misfortune that the many elements embodied in the work, and the peculiar relation they sometimes bore to the main purpose gave such ample ground for confusion and misinterpretation. There was also too apparent in the book a disregard of *former* ideas and prevailing tones of thought, if not even an ill-disguised contempt for these; and though the thorough honesty of purpose might have excused the boldness these were dealt with, yet men are seldom more ready to acknowledge defects in their systems than faults in themselves, and were but too eager to point out what looked to them as crudenesses or even as grave errors of judgment. For as Mr. Ruskin could not confine himself to the narrow line of criticism which had been formerly pursued with the utmost iteration and weary detail; but had imported into his essay the fruits of careful and extensive researches in foreign fields, there were some appearances of ground for the statement that the production was more than anything else the self-willed assertion of an eccentric and ambitious though assuredly powerful intellect. To weaken the influence of a work there never has been a more successful way than to impugn the motive which prompted its production; and this was done with due admixture of cunning praise by bands of newspaper writers and reviewers, in the case of the *Modern Painters*. Thus it came about that Mr. Ruskin was for long regarded as a man of considerable insight, originality and force, which however, it was much to be regretted, had been sadly wasted by being made the servants of several dominating pet crotchets.

There was but little reason in this conclusion regarding *Modern Painters* and its author. Even so far as it was reasonable and correct it was used blindly and for a selfish end. Mr. Ruskin was a genuine art-critic only because he was so much more than that term had formerly been held to include. He was a thorough scholar, a bold and original thinker, and a man of keen insight not only into nature and her laws, but also into human life and its manifold relations. He did not come armed with the mere foil of a few empirical rules to test the art of the day, but rather bearing, Arthur-like, the magic Excalibur of great principles, won from Nature herself by long, arduous and patient study. His first book, broadly viewed, was as we shall see more particularly afterwards a statement of the relation in which the individual stands to Nature, which topic involves properly not only the question of art, but also a consideration, more or less exhaustive, of all social phenomena, and the principles of human progress. Thus regarded, Mr. Ruskin's digressiveness is seen at once to arise from his central idea—from the starting point adopted in fact; and was not by any means the result of stray after-thoughts, or mere irregular fruitfulness of idea. Yet thus it was that to the logical minds *Modern Painters* seemed such an incongruous unsystematic mixture in which all the departments of human knowledge were most unwarrantably brought together, and instead of being mutually interpretive rather seemed to darken and perplex by their unusual proximity. It was to them as though all the elements had been set loose and walked before their eyes in a mumuring masquerade. It was the old story of the couched eye, of course, and no more. In this work lie the germs of all Mr. Ruskin's later writings in art or in political economy; indeed, these may be said to severally trace themselves to this as to a common centre and to find their roots here. I cannot therefore accept as at all correct the statement that he has wrought himself free from many of his earlier ideas. He has rather confirmed himself in these by being able to definitely develop them, with more rigour of application, into new grounds. Not a single English writer has been on the whole more consistent from first to last than Ruskin.

It is a special and distinguishing mark of the genuine thinker, and in this he differs from the merely logical one, that he gives the whole spirit of his system in every portion of it; that as he works from his character so he communicates it in every section; and that his works let them be never so complete will yet only be sections of a greater whole which may never be actually and outwardly realized, but which will still be felt to be promised and possible. Indeed it is no very good symptom when a man must constrain his truth into definite logical completeness as the one only hopeful means of recommending it to his fellows. I once heard an independent minister of note * remark that great truths were only realised through contradictions. Strange as this statement may seem it is true. It is merely a recognition of the fact that truth is vital, and that words are but the extremes or poles between which she passes—now as it were from light to shadow and again from shadow to light. If we perceive a lofty strong yet sweet human spirit calmly shining upon us through the pages of a book we need not much trouble ourselves about whether it is complete or not; indeed we may be sure it will be incomplete. The book of creation itself, in which the Creator has mirrored the outlines of his character for us to look upon with delight, is not completely opened to our view, if indeed it is in the sense we now mean a complete book. And all great human books will more or less resemble the divine one. The completeness of the spirit will shine through the breaks and rents of the form or the flesh and come the nearer to us and touch us the deeper and tenderer on this very account.

So it is in a measure with *Modern Painters*. It is a great book, because it is so full of soul. A far deeper than logical unity runs through it, like a golden thread, giving to its various parts "the bond of life." Each portion has a definite relation to the whole, which

---

* The Rev. William Pulsford, of Glasgow, formerly of Edinburgh.

is not metaphysical but rather vital and organic. The special or critical in the book was, in fact, only as a text which suggested the most original thoughts, the most glowing illustrations, the profoundest glances into social questions and the most touching and powerful pictures of life and nature.   And so we need not wonder very much that the artists were puzzled and perplexed beyond measure, and listened, wistful, to the finest passages as if to some vague subtle wind-music; nor that the critics were annoyed and chagrined, feeling as if in very truth a bombshell had been thrown unexpectedly among them.   Those more thoughtful minds again, who could have best appreciated the broader element in the work, were repelled by the too justifiable expectation of finding only another of such dry, technical, abstract treatises as had before been given forth under the specious name of art-criticism ; and we may be assured that the barren discussions about Tintoret and Turner that followed in the magazines and newspapers would not have the effect of drawing such persons any the more readily towards it.

But nevertheless it by-and-by came to be discovered that here for the first time in English literature the principles of art were clearly and with the utmost rigour of analysis shown to have their roots in human passions, desires and hopes ; and abstract formal canons of criticism once for all cast aside as inefficient and of none account.   *Modern Painters* was the signal of revolution, or more properly the deliberate carrying of a new moral reform, which had been inaugurated by Thomas Carlyle, into the sphere of painting and sculpture. The battle is not yet finished, but already several of the outposts have been gained, and the warriors are boldly extending their lines to right and left and ultimately there is no doubt the day must be theirs.

As inaugurating quite a new era of art-criticism, *Modern Painters* is valuable; yet, as has been said, far less for this than for the moral lessons applied in it from beginning to end, and the deep glances it affords into the spirit of things. Art-criticism, it is true, is here proclaimed to be no longer a mere study of form and colour, though these are of importance as media of ideas, and as symbols of natural laws; but rather a serious search for spiritual truths; and as being associated with the discussion of those deep and interesting social questions, it is found to be a matter of practical and vital concern—an attempt towards the discovery of truth and beauty, and the disentanglement of these from all contact with unworthy, ugly, and degrading forms, by the truthful and determined study of every object as a whole. Here, in one word, the author refuses to view the artist as in any respect separated from the man : serene and clear, from the inmost region of the soul, flows that stream of truth and beauty, transfiguring all that is outward and earthly. Without the infusion of this, to a greater or less extent, there is not and cannot

be any true art, however clever, finished and even gracefully laboured the handling may happen to be. To high,
even holy impulses and beautiful aspirations all art
worthy the name is traced as to hidden roots; it being
strictly required that the artist should have earnestly
lived what he paints. Art is, by the very nature of
it, earnest and religious; here there is no distinction
as between secular and sacred. It cannot in any
circumstances be made the toy of the drawing-room, or
the medium of after-dinner amusement. If entered on
at all it must be with a spirit of earnestness and self-
denial, pursued in a like frame of mind; and to be rightly
appreciated and enjoyed it must be approached with a
manful and serious disposition of thought and heart.

Mr. Ruskin's mission may be indicated in few words.
It is to recall men to a fact almost forgotten in the
midst of the great mechanical advances and material
enrichment of the age—the sacredness of individual
life. Whether we regard him as art-critic, moralist or
political economist we soon discover that to enforce and
impress this is the one end he has in view; and that to
this he has with undivided purpose consecrated his gifts,
his life. The key, in fact, to all Mr. Ruskin's writings
lies in the clear recognition of this. They will never be
properly understood and appreciated unless this idea is
carefully carried along with one in reading them.
Individuality lies in the soul. In the soul alone does
God reveal himself to man, and that only in these special

marks and peculiarities by which each man is, so to speak, distinguished from all other men. True union of men thus becomes possible by the existence and development of those wide yet gently-marked differences of character and constitution; and it is only in the measure a man is true to the unfolding of these that he is a minister of good to society and valuable, or to use Mr. Ruskin's own phrase, available to life, in it, inasmuch as it is only in the degree that this is realized that each one can become helpful to the unfolding of that which is truly " available to life" in other souls. It is by the existence of such faithfully developed individualities that society itself becomes possible. In remote places, by quiet noble lives, such men keep a stream of healthful life-giving influences flowing into the world from the unseen. Society is literally saved by their good doing. Day by day it is regenerated through their example, and refreshed by their unfailing faith. Thus at length the *Whole*, the Godlike is witnessed for and is manifested in human society,—in other words a Church is formed, the symbol of the All, whose portions first rise out of the individual, and in harmonious combination constitute a new medium of life and wealth. All art and all work of whatever kind should have for chief end the realisation of that deepest and distinctive in the soul; for this purpose were gifts of speech, representation and even capacities for ordinary day-labour given to man; and indeed it may safely be said for nothing else were they given. Any piece of art or artisanship the doing of which calls not into active exercise this vital element, is false, diseased, accursed— the source of many evils. Here we discover how it is that with Mr. Ruskin the art, which is not in its inmost spirit and purpose religious, is not accounted art at all. And we see too how it is that Mr. Ruskin, quite consistently with his whole scheme, can so decisively set down as the basis of all true political economy—respect for life. We detect here the sharp point of contact between the criticism of art and the truths of political economy, properly viewed, and know how it is that in discussing the one Mr. Ruskin has always been led to deal, more or less exhaustively, with the other also. For a human creature to develop all his various faculties and powers through the soul or from the silent force of his individual being, is freedom and blessedness; for him again to feel hampered, hemmed in, and unable to assert that individuality owing to pressure of circumstance, custom, habit, or law, is misery and in the end inevitably becomes moral death. Those in whom this heaven-given force of individuality more clearly and spontaneously unfolds itself in the face of opposition and hindrance are the guides and teachers of the race, whom it is the duty of men to regard with honour and to obey; and hence the weight which, with Ruskin, is constantly laid upon obedience to teachers and superiors; his praise of permanence in all the relations of life; and his unceasing advocacy of simplicity in taste and habit. Thus it is that he can so beautifully write :—

"I know not if a day is ever to come when the nature of right freedom will be understood, and when men will see that to obey another man, to labour for him, yield reverence to him or to his place, is not slavery. It is often the best kind of liberty,—liberty from care. The man who says to one, Go, and he goeth, and to another, Come, and he cometh, has, in most cases, more sense of restraint and difficulty than the man who obeys him. The movements of the one are hindered by the burden on his shoulder ; of the other, by the bridle on his lips : there is no way by which the burden may be lightened ; but we need not suffer from the bridle if we do not champ at it. To yield reverence to another, to hold ourselves and our lives at his disposal, is not slavery ; often, it is the noblest state in which a man can live in this world. There is, indeed, a reverence which is servile, that is to say, irrational or selfish :· but there is also noble reverence, that is to say, reasonable and loving ; and a man is never so noble as when he is reverent in this kind ; nay, even if the feeling pass the bounds of mere reason, so that it be loving, a man is raised by it. Which had, in reality, most of the serf nature in him,—the Irish peasant who was lying in wait yesterday for his landlord, with his musket muzzle thrust through the ragged hedge ; or that old mountain servant, who, 200 years ago at Inverkeithing, gave up his own life and the lives of his seven sons for his chief?—as each fell, calling forth his brother to the death, "Another for Hector!" And, therefore, in all ages and all countries, reverence has been paid and sacrifice made by men to each other, not only without complaint, but rejoicingly; and famine, and peril, and sword, and all evil, and all shame, have been borne willingly in the causes of masters and kings; for all these gifts of the heart ennobled the men who gave, not less than the men who received them, and nature prompted, and God rewarded the sacrifice. But to feel their souls withering within them, unthanked: to find their whole being sunk into an unrecognized abyss; to be counted off into a heap of mechanism, numbered with its wheels, and weighed with its hammer strokes;—this nature bade not,—this God blesses not,— this humanity for no long time is able to endure."

Out of this central idea, or life-root, we have indicated, Mr. Ruskin's philosophy runs as by necessity in a twofold shoot—the one, in short, being, man's relation to Nature; and the other, the relation of the individual to society and social regulations of whatever kind. In all his works we have, it is true, the simultaneous discussion or following out of the two branches; but in the one class the first line of inquiry is kept incidental and subordinate, and in the other the second is so. For critical purposes his writings may safely enough be divided into two classes. The first we may thus classify:

—*The Modern Painters, The Seven Lamps of Architecture, The Stones of Venice, Lectures on Painting and Architecture*, and the *Two Paths;* the second, again, we may so arrange :—the *Political Economy of Art, The Harbours of England, Unto this Last*, and *Papers on Political Economy.*

In the first phase of his teaching Mr. Ruskin through a thousand forms and by a thousand eloquent and powerful illustrations enforces upon us the doctrine that man as an art-loving and art-producing creature can only preserve his individuality and freedom by being in the highest sense true to nature. Not in slavishly copying her forms, but in reverently following her inner meanings and monitions and dwelling in constant accord with her purer spirit can he find that true enjoyment and realize that fulness of being which will enable him to express what is best and deepest in him and at the same time keep all his work alive by a gleam of gladness, freshness and serene cheerful strength. There is but one way to be original and that is simply to be true in the larger sense of it. Never was there a great picture that was not painted out of a sense of solemn joy in communion with nature, or a serene yet intense sympathy with human life—its gladnesses or its sorrows. Other recipe for being great there is none than this of being devoutly true. As Polonius has it :—

> First to thine ownself be true,
> And it must follow as the night the day,
> Thou canst not then be false to any man.

And Shakspeare might have added,—

Nor canst thou e'en be false to thing that is.

Calm patient insight guided by a steady determination after truth is the one condition of lofty art. For as painting is but a language of a nobler sort, the whole question resolves itself into the character of the artist,— what he has attained, thought, felt, been and lived. The cramped and painful copying of mere external forms is a sign of littleness or decay, inevitably producing listlessness and languor on the worker, and on the spectator a feeling of oppressive weariness and mental nightmare. As certain strong minds dominate men in the metaphysical and theological fields by imposing on them their classifications, so in art it often happens that periods of feebleness are marked by vassalage to the style and method of one man. All strong healthy periods are independent and individual; all weak unhealthy ones are characterized by the existence of scholars instead of masters, copyists instead of inventors, apologists for their time instead of ennoblers and justifiers of it. The mark of the copyist is the signal of the renunciation of freedom; in the measure that the artists have fallen under the rule of a single mind or into submission to an effete order of art, so do their productions become less and less in value to humanity, save merely as warnings and mournful examples. But the degradation of art is always preceded by a social

decline. The Greeks had long lost that healthy strength
and aptitude for nature, before their marbles declined
into dead lines; the Italians had abandoned themselves
to all excesses of licence before their pictures became in
the period of the Medicis a scandal and a shame—
denounced of the bold Savonarola as unholy and utterly
sensual. Then they were a nation of bold copyists,—
and their vigour was only in a ratio with their vice.
"And so it is always," says Ruskin. Thus speaks he
of true vigour :—" I said that the power of human mind
had its growth in the wilderness; much more must the
love and the conception of that beauty, whose every line
and hue we have seen to be, at the best a faded image
of God's daily work and an arrested ray of some star of
creation, be given chiefly in the places which He has
gladdened by planting there the fir-tree and the pine.
Not within the walls of Florence, but among the far-away
fields of her lilies, was the child trained who was to
raise that headstone of Beauty above her towers of
watch and war. Remember all that he became; count
the sacred thoughts with which he filled the heart of
Italy; ask those who followed him what they learned at
his feet; and when you have numbered his labours and
received their testimony, if it seemed to you that God
had verily poured out upon His servant no common nor
restrained portion of His Spirit, and that he was indeed
a king among the children of men, remember also
that the legend upon his crown was that of David—' I

took thee from the sheepcote and from following the sheep.'"

And thus it was that Ruskin found it quite compatible with his high notions of art so to admire the Gothic. It was rude, wild, weird to be sure ; but it bore throughout marks of freedom, and individual truth. The strange half-savage forms upon the arches and flying buttresses were uncouth, sometimes even ugly at first glance, but the idea of them had flashed direct from the mind of the producer and with little care for that false fineness of finish which is so much sought after now, he joyously threw his first idea into stone and still with wild force and expression it looks down upon us,—" children of later • times," after the lapse of centuries, with a sort of stern reproof if not reproach. For as Mr. Ruskin estimates the worth of all production by the spirit of self-sacrifice evident in it, and constantly asserts that the aim of true art is that man by it may realize his " being's chief end and aim "—to glorify God namely, it follows that that is only true and lasting that flows from the soul and is the token of a joyous childlike freedom. This idea applied to ornamentation calls forth such statements as these :—

" All ornament is base which takes for its object human work : it is utterly base,—painful to every right-toned mind, without perhaps immediate sense of the reason, but for a reason palpable enough when we do think of it. For to carve our own work and set it up for admiration, is a miserable self-complacency, a contentment in our own wretched doings, when we might have been looking at God's doings. And all noble ornament is the exact reverse of this. It is the expression of man's delight in God's work." And as if by necessity, inasmuch as Mr. Ruskin directly traces all beauty in a work to the spirit out of which it came and the mood in which it was fashioned, we have the following :—

"I believe the right question to ask, respecting all ornament, is simply this : Was it done with enjoyment —was the carver happy while he was about it? It may be the hardest work possible, and the harder because so much pleasure was taken in it; but it must have been happy too, or it will not be living. How much of the stone-mason's toil this condition would exclude I hardly venture to consider, but the condition is absolute. There is a Gothic church lately built near Rouen, vile enough, indeed, in its general composition, but excessively rich in detail; many of the details are designed with taste, and all evidently by a man who has studied old work closely. But it is all as dead as leaves in December; there is not one tender touch, not one warm stroke, on the whole façade. The men who did it hated it, and were thankful when it was done. And so long as they do so, they are merely loading your walls with shapes of clay : the garlands of everlastings in Père la Chaise are more cheerful ornaments. You cannot get the feeling by paying for it—money will not buy life. I am not sure even that you can get it by watching or waiting for it."

These passages once well understood Mr. Ruskin's predilection for the old Gothic will then be easily appreciated and accounted for.

The Gothic, indeed, stands in relation to modern architecture very much as the earlier ballads to later and more artificial poetry. The chief characteristic of both is freedom from prescribed rule—utter unconsciousness even of any outward arbitrary restraint. As the ballad presented faithfully and without reserve the feelings, impulses, thoughts of the early rover or adventurer—mirrored in fact his savage changefulness of mood and off-hand ways of dealing with his brother men, so the Gothic indicated with much the same breadth and clearness the position in which the as yet but half-cultured men stood to nature and the supernatural. For constantly from out behind the rude irregular lines of the Gothic come soft gleams of the higher and deeper—sweet glances into the sublimest region of moral and spiritual truth, just as sometimes the tenderest, most touching glimpses of soul suffuse and soften the coarse, cramped, careworn features of the poor day-worker, making the harsh scarred face "beautiful exceedingly." It is this, not any external definiteness of line as in the Greek art, which so binds each Gothic building into one harmonious whole, and imparts to it that noble universality we find nowhere else save in that literature which in the respects indicated resembles the old Gothic both in spirit and form. As the finer of our ballads, with all their wild breadth and

rugged truthfulness, yet hold firmly of that which is
purer, more permanent in human passion, longing and
life, so the Gothic, in its upheaped mountainous grandeur,
retains in its slightest wave and turn traces of the most
beautiful thoughts and deepest sympathies, like nature,
which in the farthest cranny of the jagged rock-buttress
plants her softest, sweetest-scented flowers. A Gothic
cathedral is a great ballad done in stone. It sings itself
silently through a thousand years in healthful and happy
results on the minds and hearts of men. And the reason
of its lasting and beneficial influence is this, that we see
in it the victory of united wills over rudeness of form,
restraints of life, and those elements of disorder, division
and lust which so separate man from man.

We are in the habit of thinking and of saying that ours
is the age of progress and united action. It is an age
of combination, co-operation, hardly of union. Men are
bound together by stern everyday necessities—by bodily
wants in fact, rather than by their soul-needs; all our
great mechanical achievements bearing witness to this fact
in their incompleteness, their external finery, and the
rigid constraint visible in them from foundation to top-
stone. The old Gothic in its grand individuality and
serene though stern freedom rebukes us in our very worst
tendency : and therefore we would despise it if we could.
But it forever remains true that nothing really lasts
save what is born of freedom, nursed of sympathy and
love, and trembles softly through its dark cloudy atmo-

14

sphere into clear dew of heaven. The Italian Dante lasts still, because his great world-work is essentially Gothic. It is rude and grand—irregular even in its seeming regularity; and transfigured by tenderness and severity of truth. It is a Gothic cathedral whose foundations are laid deep in the central darkness; and yet on whose roof rests the living light of Paradise. Shakspeare too was Gothic; he reared a great temple in the wild and men in all ages will go up to admire and worship in it the great figure of humanity enshrined there. Milton again loses just in so far as he was a Grecian—a great scholar—conscious at once of his powers and the rules which so hampered and hemmed him in.

Thus then we can discover why it is that Mr. Ruskin so admires the Gothic. It cannot be copied or followed save in the measure that its spirit is appropriated. In this too it resembles our ballad literature. It is so majestically true, so rich in intensely individual markings, and we may say arose full-formed spontaneous out of the great element of human yearning and human hope as Venus rose living and full-formed from the bosom of the sea.

The soul of Mr. Ruskin's art-system is self-abnegation—sorrow over human littleness and insufficiency; joy silent, unspeakable, in the fulness and truth and beauty of God. And hence the same idea is directed towards architecture:—" The difference between these two orders of building is not merely that which there is in nature between things beautiful and sublime. It is, also, the difference between what is derivative and original in man's work; for whatever is in architecture fair and beautiful, is imitated from natural forms; and what is not so derived, but depends for its dignity upon arrangement and government received from human mind, becomes the expression of the power of that mind and receives a sublimity high in proportion to the power expressed. All building, therefore, shows man either as gathering or governing; and the secrets of his success are his knowing what to gather and how to rule. These are the two great intellectual lamps of architecture; the one consisting in a just and humble veneration for the works of God upon the earth and the other in an understanding of the dominion over those which have been vested in man."

And thus throughout all there is a constant reference to the development of true life and freedom on the part of the artist or worker, and we have constantly utterances such as these :—

"We are not sent into this world to do anything into which we cannot put our hearts. We have certain work to do for our bread, and that is to be done strenuously; other work to do for our delight, and that is to be done heartily: neither is to be done by halves and shifts, but with a will; and what is not worth this effort is not to be done at all. Perhaps all that we have to do is meant for nothing more than an exercise of the heart and of the will, and is useless in itself; but, at all events, the little use it has may well be spared if it is not worth putting our hands and our strength to. It does not become our immortality to take an ease inconsistent with its authority, nor to suffer any instruments with which it can dispense, to come between it and the things it rules : and he who would form the creations of his own mind by any other instrument than his own hand, would also, if he might, give grinding organs to Heaven's angels, to make their music easier. There is dreaming enough, and earthiness enough, and sensuality enough in human existence without our turning the few glowing moments of it into mechanism ; and since our life must at the best be but a vapour that appears for a little time and then vanishes away, let it at least appear as a cloud in the height of Heaven, not as the thick darkness that broods over the blast of the Furnace, and rolling of the Wheel."

Thus from the vital point of view we see clearly how the two branches of Mr. Ruskin's scheme meet and run into each other ; and find that it is the idea of individual freedom, which furnishes the stepping-stone from the one to the other. Mr. Ruskin has himself in a few beautiful words shown the natural and necessary relation of the two, when he thus succinctly finds in the products of a great art the type of a noble life :—

" There are two characters in which all greatness of art consists :—First, the earnest and intense seizing of natural facts; then the ordering those facts by strength of human intellect, so as to make them, for all who look upon them, to the utmost serviceable, memorable, and beautiful. And thus great art is nothing else than the type of strong and noble life; for, as the ignoble person, in his dealings with all that occurs in the world about him, first sees nothing clearly,—looks nothing fairly in the face, and then allows himself to be swept away by the trampling torrent, and unescapable force, of the things that he would not foresee, and could not understand: so the noble person, looking the facts of the world full in the face, and fathoming them with deep faculty, then deals with them in unalarmed intelligence and unhurried strength, and becomes, with his human intellect and will, no unconscious nor insignificant agent in consummating their good, and restraining their evil.

" Thus in human life you have the two fields of rightful toil for ever distinguished, yet for ever associated; Truth first—plan or design, founded thereon: so in art, you have the same two fields, for ever distinguished, for ever associated; Truth first—plan or design founded thereon."

Mr. Ruskin, quite consistently with his scheme of things, seriously declines to enter fully on a definition of the utility of any object till he has discovered and determined the *use* of man himself. In one word he refuses to be abstract, or to view man in any metaphysical relation whatever. His philosophy constrains everything to measure itself by its professed living prototype; and many grand and imposing things are thus compelled to go their way as being contemptible, little and even worse than that—false, degrading and in their ultimate influence, diabolic. Other critics may content themselves with a merely arbitrary abstract classification of relations—beautiful, orderly, complete from a certain point of view; but quite inefficient to exhaust all the phenomena of life, because excluding the most vital region in human experience. Indeed it is matter of grave surprise that this one essential element should have been so long neglected as that it should have been left for Mr. Ruskin once more to assert its influence—even its existence practically; and to connect it once more in a systematic but vital way with art and political economy. Goethe, I remember, speaks somewhere about two conditions being notoriously essential to make a great epoch—a good head and a great inheritance. Napoleon, he went on to say, inherited the French Revolution, Frederick the Great the Silesian War, Luther the darkness of the Popes, and I, he added with a certain naïve touch of egotism, the errors of the Newtonian theory. So Mr. Ruskin's inheritance was the darkness of debased half-heathen theories of art and of social relations; which in presence of a professed Christianity were yet accepted and acted upon so far as men could act upon them. Perhaps one of the strangest positions society ever yet found itself in ! The result of the teachings of the political-economy doctors was a bold self-avowed materialism. Very significantly therefore Mr. Ruskin writes in the opening to his second volume of *Modern Painters* : —

" Man's use and function (and let him who will not grant me this follow me no farther, for this I purpose always to assume) are, to be the witness of the glory of God, and to advance that glory by his reasonable obedience and resultant happiness.

" Whatever enables us to fulfil this function is, in the pure and first sense of the word, Useful to us ; pre-eminently therefore, whatever sets the glory of God more brightly before us. But things that only help us to exist are, in a secondary and mean sense, useful ; or, rather, if they be looked for alone, they are useless, and worse, for it would be better that we should not exist, than that we should guiltily disappoint the purposes of existence.

" And yet people speak in this working age, when they speak from their hearts, as if houses and lands, and food and raiment, were alone useful, and as if Sight, Thought, and Admiration were all profitless, so that men insolently call themselves Utilitarians, who would turn, if they had their way, themselves and their race into vegetables ; men who think, as far as such can be said to think, that the meat is more than the life, and the raiment than the body, who look to the earth as a

stable, and to its fruit as fodder; vinedressers and
husbandmen, who love the corn they grind, and the
grapes they crush, better than the gardens of the angels
upon the slopes of Eden; hewers of wood and drawers
of water, who think that it is to give them wood to hew,
and water to draw, that the pine-forests cover the mountains like the shadow of God, and the great rivers move
like His eternity. And so come upon us that Woe of
the preacher, that though God ' hath made everything
beautiful in his time, also he hath set the world in their
heart, so that no man can find out the work that God
maketh from the beginning to the end.'

"This Nebuchadnezzar curse, that sends men to
grass like oxen, seems to follow but too closely on the
excess or continuance of national power and peace. In
the perplexities of nations, in their struggles for existence, in their infancy, their impotence, or even their
disorganization, they have higher hopes and nobler
passions. Out of the suffering comes the serious mind;
out of the salvation, the grateful heart; out of endur-
ance, fortitude; out of deliverance, faith: but when
they have learned to live under providence of laws, and
with decency and justice of regard for each other, and
when they have done away with violent and external
sources of suffering, worse evils seem to arise out of
their rest; evils that vex less and mortify more, that
suck the blood though they do not shed it, and ossify
the heart though they do not torture it. And deep

though the causes of thankfulness must be to every people at peace with others and at unity in itself, there are causes of fear, also, a fear greater than of sword and sedition : that dependence on God may be forgotten, because the bread is given and the water sure ; that gratitude to him may cease, because his constancy of protection has taken the semblance of a natural law ; that heavenly hope may grow faint amidst the full fruition of the world ; that selfishness may take place of undemanded devotion, compassion be lost in vain glory, and love in dissimulation ; that enervation may succeed to strength, apathy to patience, and the noise of jesting words and foulness of dark thoughts, to the earnest purity of the girded loins and the burning lamp. About the river of human life there is a wintry wind, though a heavenly sunshine ; the iris colours its agitation, the frost fixes upon its repose. Let us beware that our rest become not the rest of stones, which so long as they are torrent-tossed and thunder-stricken maintain their majesty, but when the stream is silent, and the storm passed, suffer the grass to cover them, and the lichen to feed on them, and are ploughed down into dust.

"And though I believe that we have salt enough of ardent and holy mind amongst us to keep us in some measure from this moral decay, yet the signs of it must be watched with anxiety, in all matters however trivial, in all directions however distant. And at this time,

when the iron roads are tearing up the surface of
Europe, as grape-shot do the sea, when their great net
is drawing and twitching the ancient frame and strength
together, contracting all its various life, its rocky arms
and rural heart, into a narrow, finite, calculating metro-
polis of manufactures; when there is not a monument
throughout the cities of Europe that speaks of old years
and mighty people, but it is being swept away to build
cafés and gaming-houses; when the honour of God is
thought to consist in the poverty of his temple, and
the column is shortened and the pinnacle shattered, the
colour denied to the casement and the marble to the
altar, while exchequers are exhausted in luxury of
boudoirs and pride of reception-rooms; when we ravage
without a pause all the loveliness of creation which God
in giving pronounced Good, and destroy without a
thought all those labours which men have given their
lives and their sons' sons' lives to complete, and have
left for a legacy to all their kind, a legacy of more than
their hearts' blood, for it is of their souls' travail; there
is need, bitter need, to bring back into men's minds,
that to live is nothing, unless to live be to know Him
by whom we live; and that He is not to be known by
marring his fair works, and blotting out the evidence
of his influences upon his creatures; not amidst the
hurry of crowds and crash of innovation, but in solitary
places, and out of the glowing intelligences which he
gave to men of old. He did not teach them how to

build for glory and for beauty, he did not give them the fearless, faithful, inherited energies that worked on and down from death to death, generation after generation, that we might give the work of their poured-out spirit to the axe and the hammer; He has not cloven the earth with rivers, that their white wild waves might turn wheels and push paddles, nor turned it up under, as it were fire, that it might heat wells and cure diseases; He brings not up his quails by the east wind, only to let them fall in flesh about the camp of men; He has not heaped the rocks of the mountain only for the quarry, nor clothed the grass of the field only for the oven."

The way in which Mr. Ruskin constantly seeks to elevate man into freedom, and Nature into beauty (by means of the purification of the moral sense) proves him truly a Christian teacher. For in the Classical nature was subdued into a merely passive instrument of enjoyment or pleasure; her beauty was only recognized in so far as it ministered to the sense, and her power was but a source of fear and terror without any relief or recommendation whatsoever. Ruskinism again is the elevation of each thing to its due and proper place as a symbol of moral truth; and a denial to it of any worth or weight apart from the moral or spiritual idea of which it is the type and the medium. In the one, Nature narrowed her beauty to what was pure in form, sweet to sense, and pleasant in use; in the other Beauty sheds its benign presence widely abroad — nestles in the common, shrouds itself in the shrill hurricane and sits serene even upon the crest of the curling tempest-driven wave. Nature to the heathen, in short, was full of peril and awe; and only beautiful in relation to the body: to the Christian she is great in the lowly, the common, the remote, because all are expressions of God's attributes and channels through which He speaks to the soul of mankind. In the constant assertion of this truly Christian idea of art and work, Mr. Ruskin establishes for himself an independent place in the literature of his country.

But if Mr. Ruskin deserves our hearty acknowledgments for services as an original thinker, it behoves us also to recognize thankfully the readiness with which, especially in his more recent efforts, he has stept down to the rank of an interpreter, when by so doing it seemed to him the cause of Goodness and Truth would be advanced. It has been well said that it requires an original mind to borrow rightly. It might as reasonably be asserted that towards honest interpretation a great mind is essential. Not only has Mr. Ruskin, with that clearness of insight and delicacy of analysis which always characterize him, directed us to the true meaning, and by consequence revealed to us the beauty, of many of the more obscure passages in Wordsworth, Scott, Shakspeare, and more especially Dante, of whom he seems to have made a perfect study; but he has taken on himself the more generous and to us far more important labour of interpreting from one point of view our spiritual athlete—Thomas Carlyle. Influences from this great light-centre of thought are seen from the first to mingle themselves with the outflow of Ruskin's reflections, often imparting tone, strength and quality. When one says that Mr. Ruskin has been deeply influenced by Carlyle he does not in the least detract from his merits as an original thinker. Originality indeed may be defined as the power rightly to use and to apply. It is not the mere silkworm-like spinning out of fine individual thoughts from a man's brain. Coleridge in that point of view was perhaps the most original man we have had; and yet he was probably about the least useful or available. Originality consists with due recognition of a master, and indeed may be said to have its main root in that. Reverence is the foundation of greatness in all the phases of it; and reverence to be of avail must be directed not towards abstractions, but living persons. It has been asserted that there is not in this country a reading, thinking man under the age of forty who has not been directly or indirectly influenced by Thomas Carlyle and has not learned from him. Indeed it may be safely said that one-half the thought of the present day is due solely to this man, whose name nevertheless some writers who have managed to establish for themselves a tolerable reputation by strutting in borrowed feathers, seem afraid to mention lest it should

too directly suggest a journey to the fountain-head.
Tithonus, Tennyson tells us, in the midst of his sad
musings sometimes doubted his own identity. He
sings :—

> With what other eyes
> I used to watch—if I be he that watched—

which lines seem capable of being so parodied as to
express the dim feelings of a certain class of our more
popular writers who would only with justice be doomed
to read Mr. Ruskin's political economy and nothing else
till they fully awakened to his ideas of honesty and
right.

But Mr. Ruskin in his consciousness of strength is
not ashamed to honestly acknowledge indebtedness. He
has received high impulses from Carlyle and he says so
plainly. We can trace it for ourselves through all his
books. It sings itself as a low murmuring accom-
paniment in the *Modern Painters*; rises to a somewhat higher pitch in the *Stones of Venice* and the *Seven
Lamps*; as he begins to grapple more firmly with
the broader problems of life it becomes more and
more decided; and in his recent essays on political
economy it comes forth in full and pellucid stream.
These last seem, indeed, to a student of Carlyle, to
be but reflections of the master's great thoughts; but
then they are reflections from a right level truthful
mirror—a mirror with no cracks or flaws—fit to give
out a fair and faithful image of whatever is presented

to it. Mr. Ruskin's great merit in these essays, as he himself so well knows and feels, is simply that he has accomplished this—that he has applied and illustrated in a simple but clear and systematic way the thoughts which in looser form Carlyle has made it his life-business to proclaim and to promulgate.

These essays on political economy—the first four of which have been republished from the *Cornhill Magazine* under the strange but significant title of *Unto this Last,* and the rest of which are appearing at considerable intervals of time in *Fraser*—belong decidedly to the highest order of Christian literature. The main truths, it is admitted, are old. They are even to be found scattered through some of the works of our earlier English writers — Sir Thomas Browne's *Christian Morals,* Hooker's *Ecclesiastical Polity,* and Jeremy Taylor's discourses, for instance. They are, as I have said, expressed with the utmost force and skill in *Sartor Resartus, Past and Present,* and the *Latter-day Pamphlets.* But here for the first time they are gathered into definite connected form and are enforced with that clearness and piercing power of words which belong to Ruskin almost alone of English writers. The essays may well be titled *Applied Christianity.* Few works of any period better deserve the title.

The exclusion from the field of political economy of that element of affection and self-denial, on which Christianity is based and which is professedly accepted as the life-guidance of this nation, could not but seem to Carlyle and Ruskin, as indeed it will to any who chooses to reflect upon it, an anomalous thing, if there ever was one. Practically to reject, in all matters of every day, those sublime doctrines the knowledge of which essentially distinguishes us from the poor pagan, whom in our conceit we incline to regard as having only lived and died that we might the easier be borne aloft heavenward, is about the most contradictory of all possible positions for human creatures to hold and to live by. And yet that is what we have done. Not only have we selfishly pursued our own course in silence and sometimes with a tinge of shame ; but men —the highest products of the age, so at least by general consent regarded, have devoted their lives to make of our practice a scientific system, no less—to establish for us a "science of selfishness." Mr. Carlyle in his *Pig Philosophy* has, in a wildly satirical yet deeply serious style, carried that sort of economy to its last issue, exploded it in point of fact ; with such trenchant and fiery sarcasm indeed that it may well be matter of surprise that a single volume of " scientific selfishness" should have since been given to the world.

Mr. Ruskin's idea is that any scheme of political economy, which shall not in its practical issues prove suicidal, must connect itself with that very root of affection which had hitherto by economists been regarded merely as a " disturbing cause ; " and in fact must take its rise from there. The stone which the builders rejected, becomes with him the chief of the corner. The despised element, disturbing cause, or however it be named, is the very basis of his system. If you inquire of him what wealth is, he proves to you with a rigour of logic, as exhaustive as that of Fichte, the absolute truth of Carlyle's seer-like words—that " the wealth of a nation is not the quantity of bullion it has realized ; but the quantity of heroisms it has achieved, of noble pieties and valiant wisdoms that were in it—that still are in it." If again you ask what value consists in he replies, " It is that which avails for life ; " and thus in every way he connects old ideas with vital and eternal facts of human experience. Mr. Ruskin's political economy is gathered up in little, as if unto a dewdrop reflecting a whole world, in this short extract from the conclusion of *Modern Painters*, which shows too that the study of this branch of science has from of old been a loved occupation of his :—

" Co-relative with the assertion, ' There is a foolish God,' is the assertion, ' There is a brutish man.' ' As no laws but those of the Devil are practicable in the world, so no impulses but those of the brute ' (says the modern political economist) ' are appealable to in the world. Faith, generosity, honesty, zeal, and self-sacrifice are poetical phrases. None of these things can, in reality be counted upon ; there is no truth in man which can be used as a moving or productive

15

power. All motive force in him is essentially brutish, covetous, or contentious. His power is only power of prey : otherwise than the spider, he cannot design ; otherwise than the tiger, he cannot feed.' This is the modern interpretation of that embarrassing article of the Creed, ' the communion of saints.'

"It has always seemed strange to me, not indeed that this creed should have been adopted, it being the entirely necessary consequence of the previous fundamental article ;—but that no one should ever seem to have any misgivings about it ;—that, practically, no one had *seen* how strong work *was* done by man ; how either for hire, or for hatred, it never had been done ; and that no amount of pay had ever made a good soldier, a good teacher, a good artist, or a good workman. You pay your soldiers and sailors so many pence a day, at which rated sum, one will do good fighting for you ; another bad fighting. Pay as you will, the entire goodness of the fighting depends, always, on its being done for nothing ; or rather, less than nothing, in the expectation of no pay but death. Examine the work of your spiritual teachers, and you will find the statistical law respecting them is, ' The less pay, the better work.' Examine also your writers and artists : for ten pounds you shall have a Paradise Lost, and for a plate of figs, a Dürer drawing ; but for a million of money sterling, neither. Examine your men of science : paid by starvation, Kepler will discover the laws of the orbs of heaven for you ;—and, driven out to die in the street, Swammerdam shall discover the laws of life for you—such hard terms do they make with you, these brutish men, who can only be had for hire.

"Neither is good work ever done for hatred, any more than hire ;—but for love only. For love of their country, or their leader, or their duty, men fight steadily ; but for massacre and plunder, feebly. Your signal, 'England expects every man to do his duty,' they will answer ; your signal of black flag and death's head, they will not answer. And verily they will answer it no more in commerce than in battle. The cross bones will not make a good shop-sign, you will find ultimately, any more than a good battle-standard. Not the cross bones, but the cross.

"Now the practical result of this infidelity in man, is the utter ignorance of all the ways of getting his right work out of him. From a given quantity of human power and intellect, to produce the least possible result, is a problem solved, nearly with mathematical precision, by the present methods of the nation's economical procedure. The power and intellect are enormous. With the best soldiers, at present existing, we survive in battle, and but survive, because, by help of Providence, a man whom we have kept all his life in command of a company forces his way at the age of seventy so far up as to obtain permission to save us, and die, unthanked. With the shrewdest thinkers in the world, we have not yet succeeded in arriving at any national conviction respecting the uses of life."

Nothing I may remark, has more deeply impressed me during a recent careful re-reading of Mr. Ruskin's works than the perfect homogeneousness which marks them and unites them together, notwithstanding their apparent diffuseness. And as it is with all, so with each. In those essays, for instance, there is properly no theorizing; completeness is not gained by any trick or intellectual bye-play; but flows rather from the hold laid on a few simple principles, out of which all the manifold lines of relation may be said to spring as naturally and necessarily as branches from the trunk of a tree. Mr. Ruskin does not work merely from a survey of facts outside him, though those too have their due place assigned them; but from a deeper region of law, eternal as the Divine Being himself; and through his firm hold on this he is enabled to propound a solution for the social problems of the time. To understand these essays no acuteness of intellect, or previous statistical study is required; but simply solid sense and openness of mind and heart. Impossible! Utopian! one can easily imagine to be the epithets with which Mr. Ruskin's scheme would be met by many. Not altogether so, I answer. Were there not a sphere in society where Mr. Ruskin's "ideal" had already realized itself in the rude way "ideals" are in the habit of realizing themselves in this world, society would not continue possible at all. It is because Mr. Ruskin's doctrines have been the guiding lights of life for the select few faithful and valiant ones, that we are now in condition even to read the unchristian trash that deluges the land about *Economy* and the *Rights of Man*. One might appeal from books to the experience of the individual reader; and ask him whether he has never met with some humble, silent, industrious soul, who would rather lose a twenty-pound note than speak an untruth, or suffer great pain personally rather than wrong his neighbour, or who altogether innocent of *Ricardo* and *Adam Smith*, would not quite proceed on the " supply and demand " principle when he wanted work done? If he has not then I can joyously call myself luckier and happier than he how rich soever he be, for I have met such men living sublime simple lives of love and faith beyond the Grampians and Hills of Dee. And I believe moreover that could we search out England we would meet with a handful of such whose everyday practice would prove beyond dispute that Mr. Ruskin's ideas are not Utopian wholly; are not impracticable, and moreover are not uneconomical. Mr. Ruskin only appeals to the " possibilities " to which Christ and his disciples appealed, lovingly and sternly by turns; and if Mr. Ruskin's scheme is Utopian and impossible then we may just as well turn our Bibles into locomotive fodder, our churches into spinning-mills, and our higher schools into shops for gingerbread and sweet-meats.

But let us thank God and take heart of grace. Mr. Ruskin, to the honour of our race be it said, does not paint a wholly Utopian society, else had all our philanthropists struggled in vain, our apostles witnessed and our martyrs suffered for nought. He only calls men back to those everlasting principles of love and truth, by the practical exhibition of which alone can men continue to live and work together in any degree of harmony and happiness. If the heroic Agamemnon is miserable and loses his force of manhood because the cunning Thersites has differed from him and shows as he best can his contempt for Agamemnon, how incalculably frightful must be the loss of energy, the waste of *wealth*, of human life and possibility caused in these days by the heart-burnings, the bickerings, the grudges maintained between class and class and man and man. It is awful to think of. Political economists had it seems wholly forgotten this consideration. Mr. Ruskin deals with it and can suggest a remedy. Our other physicians could only prescribe on the principle that " one devil will drive out another."

The low platform of common justice is that from which Mr. Ruskin works; he seeks no high-flown virtues and benevolences, but this mere justice once strictly and sternly regarded, the basis of all reformation in society is accomplished, and those relations which are regarded as the most distant and the most common are invested with a certain paternal and holy character.

The idea of the following short paragraph is, I fancy, recognized by all in a somewhat speculative way, but the practical admission of it might modify in many ways the theories and schemes of economists :—

" Absolute justice is indeed no more attainable than absolute truth ; but the righteous man is distinguished from the unrighteous by his desire and hope of justice, as the true man from the false by his desire and hope of truth. And though absolute justice be unattainable as much justice as we need for all practical use is attainable by all those who make it their aim."

I remember reading in an essay written by an American thinker a rather mystical sentence, which, however, finds beautiful illustration in a great deal that Mr. Ruskin has written. The American says :— " Let us follow *justice* in the regeneration till the low and common, as well as the wonderful, be lost in the paternal." Strange as it might appear, that sentence may be taken as the text of Mr. Ruskin's economy.

In the first of the essays, Mr. Ruskin inquires how it is that the merchant, notwithstanding his useful and peaceful avocation, has uniformly been put by society in respect of honour beneath the soldier whose trade is slaying ; and he finds the reason lies in the fact that the merchant is presumed always to act selfishly. And if any one will thoughtfully read over the rest of that

essay, in which Mr. Ruskin sets down the true functions
of the merchant in relation to his country, those he
deals with, and the individuals under his charge, he will
at once see why the sentence from the American has
been noted as the text of Mr. Ruskin's scheme of
things.

Mr. Ruskin's doctrine of fixed wages has been
regarded as very heterodox, and quite unattainable.
Mr. Ruskin has himself given a number of cases; but
practically taken, are not all those movements of trades'
unions and the still more ominous phenomena of strikes,
with which political economists as they go have such
difficulty, only vague ill-directed endeavours after some
such fixed regulation as Mr. Ruskin recommends? I
do not find that practically people distinguish between
good and bad work nearly so much as they ought; they
are influenced by a host of considerations—some circumstantial, some sentimental, as to who shall have the
privilege of their work or patronage; but these considerations very seldom indeed have reference to *justice*, or to
the effect their decision will have, not only upon the
single individual getting the work, but on crowds of
others involved.   A passage *àpropos* suggests itself
from the *Latter-day Pamphlets*.   Carlyle there says :—
"On the whole, what a reflection is it that we cannot
bestow on an unworthy man any particle of our benevolence, our patronage, or whatever resource is ours,—
without withdrawing it, it and all that will grow of it,

from one worthy, to whom it of right belongs! We
cannot, I say; impossible; it is the eternal law of
things. Incompetent Duncan McPastehorn, the hapless incompetent mortal to whom I give the cobbling of
my boots,—and cannot find in my heart to refuse it, the
poor drunken wretch having a wife and ten children;
he *withdraws* the job from sober, plainly competent and
meritorious Mr. Sparrowbill, generally short of work
too; discourages Sparrowbill; teaches him that he too
may just as well drink and loiter and bungle; that this
is not a case for merit and demerit at all, but for
dupery, and whining flattery and incompetent bungling
of every description;—clearly tending to the ruin of
poor Sparrowbill! What harm had Sparrowbill done
to me that I should so help to ruin him? And I could
not *save* the insalvable McPastehorn; I merely yielded
him for insufficient work, here and there a half-crown,—
which he oftenest drank. And now Sparrowbill also is
drinking! Justice, Justice: wo betides us everywhere
when, for this reason or for that, we fail to do justice!
No beneficence, benevolence, or other virtuous contribu-
tion will make good that want. And in what a rate of
terrible geometrical progression, far beyond *our* poor
computation, any act of injustice once done by us grows;
rooting itself ever anew, spreading ever anew, like a
banyan-tree,—blasting all life under it, for it is a poison-
tree! There is but one thing needed for the world;
but that one is indispensable. Justice, justice, in the

name of Heaven; give us justice, and we live; give us only counterfeits of it or succedanea for it and we die!"

Mr. Ruskin's notion of the result of fixed wages it is not difficult to discover. The McPastehorns have only a chance of being employed by doing work at a cheaper rate than the Sparrowbills—giving bungled semblances instead of honest work. Once fix the rate of pay, and then by meanly underselling, all hope of employment for the insalvable McPastehorns, in all departments, is gone—till they reform themselves. Employers of labour would thus be forced to discriminate more closely between good work and bad work and then there would be far fewer complaints heard about people being cheated. The result of a system of fixed wages I believe would be one of the greatest moral reforms of this or any former age.

As has already been said there is in these essays a logic far deeper than the logic of the ordinary political economy. It is a logic of vital and necessary relation, not one of abstract and formal correctness; so that those who come here, seeking logical treatises, are sure to be disappointed, and to find not only what they would term inconsistency and contradiction, but probably the strangest of paradoxes. But in every individual sentence they will find, if they look a little deeper, the expression of a character which dwells in the reverence of a deep and enduring principle, which were it carried thoroughly into the lives of men would regenerate the world. The so-called political economist again who seeks to establish a system, is only imposing upon other men's minds a new classification of relations, which had become a necessity to him, it may be, through a peculiarity or limitedness of nature and which will necessarily be partial and conflicting, however complete and consistent it may appear, from his individual point of view. But life is not a system of rules, which can be classified and packed into exact and mechanical order. " Subsists no law of life outside of life." Therefore the true economist is not so much he who builds up a new system as the man who endeavours to call mankind back to the power of those old laws, which are so simple as to be often forgotten and departed from just because of their commonness. Theory succeeds theory, and the world goes on much the same as before, reaping on the whole but little benefit from that sort of labour ; and we are thankful when a man comes speaking a word instinct with feeling and life, and fitted to make our hearts stronger, our hands readier, and our pulses to beat with a more manly stroke, because, helping us to realize rightly our high position as workers and producers. It is no new system Mr. Ruskin seeks to impose ; the truly wise man never seeks to do this, esteeming ideas and notions as of slight importance compared with the actual practice of men and the general spirit of their life. The clamour for new ideas, and the appetite for anything that has a smack of novelty, is characteristic of

an unsound and fevered age, constantly seeking help
from something outward and circumstantial, from which
no lasting health or strength can possibly proceed.

Perhaps Christian truth was never more beautifully
and powerfully applied than in the following :—

"For us, at all events, her [wisdom's] work must
begin at the entry of the doors; all true economy is
'Law of the house.' Strive to make that law strict,
simple, generous; waste nothing, and grudge nothing.
Care in nowise to make more of money, but care to
make much of it; remembering always the great,
palpable, inevitable fact—the rule and root of all
economy—that what one person has another cannot
have; and that every atom of substance, of whatever
kind, used or consumed, is so much human life spent;
which, if it issue in the saving present life, or gaining
more, is well spent, but if not, is either so much life
prevented, or so much slain. In all buying, consider,
first, what condition of existence you cause in the
producers of what you buy; secondly, whether the
sum you have paid is just to the producer, and in due
proportion, lodged in his hands; thirdly, to how much
clear use, for food, knowledge, or joy, this that you
have bought can be put; and fourthly, to whom and
in what way it can be most speedily and serviceably
distributed; in all dealings whatsoever insist on entire
openness and stern fulfilment; and in all doings, on
perfection and loveliness of accomplishment; especially

on fineness and purity of all marketable commodity;
watching at the same time for all ways of gaining, or
teaching, powers of simple pleasure; and of showing
that the sum of enjoyment depended not on the
quantity of things tasted, but on the vivacity and
patience of taste.

"And if, on due and honest thought over these
things, it seems that the kind of existence to which
men are now summoned by every plea of pity and claim
of right, may, for some time at least, not be a luxurious
one;—consider whether, even supposing it guiltless,
luxury would be desired by any of us, if we saw clearly
at our sides the suffering which accompanies it in the
world.   Luxury is indeed possible in the future—
innocent and exquisite; luxury for all, and by the help
of all; but luxury at present can only be enjoyed by the
ignorant; the cruelest man living could not sit at his
feast, unless he sat blindfold.   Raise the veil boldly;
face the light; and if, as yet, the light of the eye can
only be through tears, and the light of the body through
sackcloth, go thou forth weeping, bearing precious
seed, until the time come, and the kingdom, when
Christ's gift of bread, and bequest of peace shall be
Unto this last as unto thee; and when, for earth's
severed multitudes of the wicked and the weary, there
shall be holier reconciliation than that of the narrow
home, and calm economy, where the Wicked cease—
not from trouble, but from troubling—and the Weary

are at rest." Or this again as to True Wealth :—
" Since the essence of wealth consists in power over
men, will it not follow that the nobler and the more in
number the persons over whom it has power, the greater
the wealth ? Perhaps it may even appear after some
consideration, that the persons themselves *are* the
the wealth—that these pieces of gold, with which we are
in the habit of guiding them, are, in fact, nothing more
than a kind of Byzantine harness or trappings, very
glittering and beautiful in barbaric sight, wherewith we
bridle the creatures ; but that if these same living
creatures could be guided without the fretting and
jingling of the Byzants in their mouths and ears, they
might themselves be more valuable than their bridles.
In fact, it may be discovered that the true veins of
wealth are purple—and not in Rock, but in Flesh—
perhaps even that the final outcome and consummation
of all wealth is in the producing as many as possible
full-breathed, bright-eyed, and happy-hearted human
creatures. Our modern wealth, I think, has rather a
tendency the other way ;—most political economists
appearing to consider multitudes of human creatures
not conducive to wealth, or at best conducive to it only
by remaining in a dim-eyed and narrow-chested state
of being.

" Nevertheless, it is open, I repeat, to serious
question, which I leave to the reader's pondering,
whether, among national manufactures, that of Souls of

a good quality may not at last turn out a quite leadingly lucrative one ? Nay, in some far-away and yet undreamt-of hour, I can even imagine that England may cast all thoughts of possessive wealth back to the barbaric nations among whom they first arose; and that, while the sands of the Indus and adamant of Golconda may yet stiffen the housings of the charger, and flash from the turban of the slave, she, as a Christian mother, may at last attain to the virtues and the treasures of a Heathen one, and be able to lead forth her Sons, saying,—

" ' These are MY jewels.' "

Mr. Ruskin's great services to the country it would not be easy to estimate. He has raised the tone of appreciation of art ; more than that, he has drawn artists from subjects of a merely fantastic or fanciful character to those which are real and true in the larger sense ; and he has done much to teach all men the sacredness of *work*, however lowly or even mean it may appear to be. He is no recluse, occupied in the contemplation of dead forms, but a man of large heart, whose sympathy is generous, and whose passionate wish is to unite the brotherhood of art in no sectarian or narrow bond, but as impressed by the greatness and humanity of their calling. Mr. Ruskin has been called a man of detail—but this is not true in a proper sense, the spirit in which he enters on their contemplation being quite incompatible with the idea of assigning to details more than a subordinate place. On the other hand, in his eyes, nothing is contemptible, or even insignificant that God has made, and nothing unworthy of art that has been or may be sanctified by the association of holy thoughts, pure life, or great emotion.

The spirit of faith and reverence which springs out of this and in which Mr. Ruskin habitually writes is also well worthy of note here, when one only recurs in thought to the barren half-sceptical nonsense which prior to his advent passed for art-criticism. A calm elevated enthusiasm has grown out of this habit of devout contemplation, in the very glance of which all flippancy and scepticism stands exposed and rebuked. With the listless impassive indifference which has become a kind of fashion he is sternly severe as we might suppose an old Puritan to have been; and though it may assume to be never so respectable and religious that will not shield it from his dignified denunciation. But only let a man, however humble, be but devout and reverent, and he leads us to respect and love him; in his view all forms are sacred and beautiful so long as there is life beating in them and keeping them kindly and human. With the metaphysical he has no sympathy; he hates all that is dry and abstract. During a whole life of earnest and manly endeavour, he has preached forth the dignity of work and workmen, denouncing the present system of contracts, whereby the workman is constantly becoming, as it were, only a

portion of a great machine, and robbed of his individual
influence and freedom. He has shown that society, by
patronising mere imitations and fostering fantastic
tastes, has deprived itself of all true and simple enjoyment. What he advocates is a return to the simplicity
and aptitude for work of our fathers as the only way to
relieve the boundless *ennui* which will soon rest on
every workman's heart if these cold and mechanical
tendencies are not met and removed. For no evil
passes unavenged. It has been well said that, if you
fix a chain round the neck of a slave, the other end fixes
itself on you; and this, according to Ruskin, would
represent the relation in which the higher classes stand
to the necessitous worker. Like some of the Eastern
Nawabs, it has, by its false and frippery tastes, fixed a
heavy chain round its neck, and in vain endeavoured to
persuade itself that it was an ornament instead of a
heavy unmanageable drag; and thus, in its fevered
haste, it rushes from one extreme to another, drawing
no healthy and fruitful influence from anything, and
in its very "enjoyment languishes in desire." Mr.
Ruskin has taught us once more the time-worn truth
that happiness is far cheaper than men are willing to
believe would they only be persuaded to go to the right
merchant for it; and has thus pointed us along the
road to real wealth where we will find for fellow-
passengers that pure and beautiful trio—Contentment,
Industry, and Duty.

16

I cannot take leave of the subject without referring to the selections from Mr. Ruskin's works
which have been published in one volume by Messrs.
Smith, Elder and Co. In that adventure I am convinced that the interests of the public were first of all
consulted. Anxious that the thousands who have no
means of access to Mr. Ruskin's works should yet have
an opportunity of making acquaintance with him, the
selector evidently set about his task *con amore*. The
very cream of Mr. Ruskin's multifarious writings has
been gathered up here in little space. The gems,
which before were lost because of their being so thickly
set and so variegated, are now presented single and in
their simplicity, so that they can be each one judged in
and by itself. Such a selection was greatly needed, for
the mere size of Mr. Ruskin's books would, no doubt,
frighten some from beginning the study of his works ;
and one is glad to see that it has been so admirably
done. It was no easy matter to wander through a
garden where there was so much variety and magnifi-
cence as even to bewilder and confuse, and yet to gather
a bouquet of harmonious colours and proportions. But
this has been accomplished—the selections showing a
great deal of discrimination and taste. A certain
coherence and connection has been observed in the
arrangement ; for the selector has entered thoroughly
into the meaning and purpose of the author, and has

been able to give a oneness to the whole, so that you read on from page to page with a certain feeling of an underlying continuity of thought. He has, so to speak, opened a few eyeholes in the wall which has hitherto hid Mr. Ruskin from the mass of reading Englishmen, so that now a pretty clear glimpse of his spiritual life may be obtained, if no full and complete survey be possible. It is well surely that each one be free to fill his pitcher at a fountain which has for long been sending forth such rich and refreshing streams, and to distribute it within the circle of his own influence. It is hoped this selection may be more and more widely read; and find a place on many a working man's shelf along with the works of Robertson of Brighton, and Mr. Maurice—good friends of the people both. And with this last good wish I take leave of the subject.

ADDENDA.

HISTORICAL CHRISTIANITY.

SOME people of the very keen logical cast, I am very well aware, would be ready to point out a lurking contradiction or inconsistency in the text here. They would remind me, doubtless, that the most historical of all systems is the Christian—that more than any other it depends for its power over the memories and hearts of men on the direct testimony borne to it by the doings and especially the miracles of its Sacred Founder, when he walked about on earth at once "a glory" and a reproof to our race. While willing to admit that those facts on which the greatest stress has been laid in order to logically establish His Divine claims are of vast importance, it may yet be permitted me to point out that it was quite on other facts of a more spiritual, properly mystical, or at all events strictly individual character that He himself always sought to base his essential claims as a Divine teacher. "If they believe not Moses and the prophets, neither will they believe though one rose from the dead." And again when speaking to the disciples of removing mountains, He said, referring to conversion—"Greater miracles than these shall ye do." Indeed, it is a most remarkable fact, and one that has been sadly missed sight of by those who have written logical treatises on "Miracles" and "Evidences of Christianity," that conversion, the true all-including miracle, preceded historical miracle proper—that Peter and Andrew were called and followed our Saviour before water was turned into wine, lepers cleansed or the dead raised up. When this fact is considered thoughtfully, it might then perhaps occur to one whether it is not possible that our Lord's miracles have another purpose than conversion. At this point the quaintly-expressed desire of Sir Thomas Browne to have been born under the dispensation of the Patriarchs, that he might have had some room for the exercise of his faith, suggests itself, and it is certainly not without meaning for the people who reason logically from the miracles, if they would only for a little time exercise faculties a degree loftier in character than the logical ones.

That mystical union with the Father which permitted no form of logical proof because it scorned all reference to tests of reason, which could present no evidence

higher than its own holy presence, and by its mere presence condemned the Jews for seeking after a sign, was
the great all-including fact in which miracles, or, indeed,
anything involving the idea of the assertion of an out-
go of conscious personality, was swallowed up. To
discern its presence was matter not of the universal
reason, but of the individual heart and conscience.
And so it remains. In one very strict and very deeply
significant sense, Christianity, though influencing the
history of the world, yet itself remains unhistorical—
a thing appealing purely to the individual soul, and
resting its claims for reception upon those mystical
relations which underlie, and yet remove themselves
away from contact with, all those civil and political
elements which make up the body of public history.
As we are bound to believe that a true church still
exists in the world, so we are bound to believe that the
spirit of all miracle is still powerfully present with men
—a fact which is tacitly admitted when even two or
three meet for worship, when they pray together, and
when, above all, a specially anointed servant of God
stands up to proclaim the Gospel of Reconciliation.
Thus the age of miracles still exists; and while
we are talking or writing eloquently of "miracles"
in the past, we might and ought to be doing
"greater miracles than these" in the living present.
But here as elsewhere, men are apt to take form for
spirit, shadow for substance, Time for Eternity, and thus

to excuse themselves by pretext of knowledge and subtlety of intellect from the exercise of that self-denial and living faith which is ever evidence of the existence of the spiritual and miraculous in the lives of men. The following passage is not without reference to this point :—" The life of that Divine Man stands in no connection with the general history of the world in his time. It was a private life : his teaching was a teaching for individuals. What has publicly befallen vast masses of people, and the minor parts which compose them, belongs to the general history of the world ; what inwardly befalls individuals again belongs to such a religion as Christ taught and practised, so long as He went about upon the earth." Schiller, too, has a meaning, when he sings :—

> Only miracles can lead
> To the land of miracles.

FRIEDRICH WILHELM.

GOETHE said somewhere that enthusiasm was the one thing necessary to history. It may be asserted that a reader can only comprehend that one simple lesson or great idea Carlyle so constantly enforces, in the measure that he shares the enthusiasm the biographer of Friedrich uniformly cherishes toward the subject treated of. A leisurely and careful re-perusal of *Friedrich* has once more seriously borne this in upon my mind. It has convinced me, moreover, of the correctness of the interpretation of the Hero-worship given in the text. I have resolved it into an intense admiration of the careful and skilful direction of those more generally attainable elements of patience, order, economy, prudence, and sincerity to the facts of life, as opposed properly to ideas which tend to set up as heroic those morbid and practically unavailable developments of special and peculiar faculties with which the mass of men have nothing whatever in common. A convincing proof of the truth of this might be found in Carlyle's treatment of Friedrich Wilhelm, who was

certainly one of the most heroic and remarkable of men,
—judged from this, perhaps somewhat low point of
view,—history has to tell of. The brilliant soldierly
achievements of the son scarcely deserved to cast into
the shade to such an extent as they have done the *manly*
and thoroughly heroic qualities of the father. For, as
in some other cases I have in the course of the Essay
referred to, the father is doubtless the greater character of
the two, although circumstances combined to make the
son the most historical.

It is not unlikely, I think, that Carlyle, when he
chose Friedrich the Great as his chief modern hero,
was not so familiar with the still greater father, as he
soon necessarily became in the course of close and
assidious investigation, and finding him so much a man
to his mind in every particular, he rightly resolved to
write a full and faithful history of him. Hence, we
have six volumes instead of the four originally contem-
plated, the first two being taken up with a completely
detailed biography of the grim old king, who yet had a
well of silent sweetness hidden in the heart of his rude,
unkempt, lion-like strength. At all events, I am quite
certain of this, that Friedrich Wilhelm's history, on the
whole, better illustrates Carlyle's scheme than does that
of the fighting son. Neither in ancient nor modern
history, perhaps, could Carlyle have found a better type.
Old gruff Friedrich,—with his rigorous economics, un-
yielding and exacting as nature itself; his grim-resolute

Protestantism; his stubborn, hastily-outflashing hatred of sham, idleness, French finery, and upholstery, in their many kinds, and his numerous solid, deep-based, but mostly *unconscious* virtues,—is just such an one as a student of Carlyle could fancy the master had drawn his system from patient observation of, instead of its being so otherwise. "In his boyhood," Carlyle tells us, "there was once a grand embroidered cloth-of-gold, or otherwise supremely magnificent, little Dressing-gown given him; but he would at no rate put it on, or be concerned with it; on the contrary, he stuffed it indignantly 'into the fire;' and demanded wholesome duffel instead." This was physiognomic. At the death of his father—Friedrich the First—he behaves just in such manner. From sheer filial respect he wears the French peruke till the funeral is over, then dismisses it forevermore. Scarcely is his father's body in the dust, when, as he has *already* given warning, he pays off the crowd of lazy, useless, court lackeys and gold-sticks, till only some eight or so are left. Then he goes over the pension list, and every department of the household with such Rhadamanthine resolution after reduction to a minimum, that the whole expenses are reduced to below a fifth of what they had been—55,000 thalers instead of 276,000. And he does precisely the same with the public departments; sets on foot new and better methods of farming his own domain-lands; and will not on any account cheat or permit cheating. And so he proceeds till at length *Saxon* professors set to lecturing on his doings and him, whom they designate " der grosse Wirth (great Manager, Husbandryman, or Landlord) of the Epoch." Carlyle remarks that for the first ten years of his reign, he had a great struggle with his finance, and rescuing other branches of administration from "strangling im-broglios of coiled nonsense, and put upon a rational footing." "His labour in these years," he goes on to say, "must have been great; the pushing and pulling strong and continual. The good plan itself, this comes not of its own accord; it is the fruit of 'genius' *(which means transcendent capacity of taking trouble, first of all)*: given a huge stack of tumbled thrums, it is not in your sleep that you will find the vital centre of it, or get the first thrum by the end! And then the execution, the realising, amid the contradiction, silent and expressed, of men and things? Explosive violence was by no means Friedrich Wilhelm's method; the amount of slow, stubborn, broad-shouldered strength, in all kinds, expended by the man, strikes us as very great. The amount of patience even, though patience is not reckoned his forte." . . . . "He urged dili-gence on all mortals, would not have the very Apple-women sit 'without knitting' at their stalls, and brandished his stick, or struck it fiercely down over the incorrigibly idle:—All this, as well as his ludicrously explosive and unreasonable violence, is on record con-

cerning Friedrich Wilhelm, though it is to the latter
chiefly that the world has directed its unwise attention,
in judging of him. He was a very arbitrary king. But
then a good deal of his *arbitrium*, or sovereign will, was
that of the Eternal Heavens as well; and did exceedingly behove to be done, if the Earth would prosper.
Which is an immense consideration in regard to his
sovereign will and him! He was prompt with his
rattan in urgent cases; had his gallows also, prompt
enough, where needful. Let him see that no mistakes
happen, as certainly he means that none shall!

" Yearly he made his country richer : and this not
in money alone (which is of very uncertain value, and
sometimes has no value at all, and even less), but in
frugality, diligence, punctuality, veracity,—the grand
fountains from which money and all real *values* and
valours spring for men. To Friedrich Wilhelm, in
his rustic simplicity, money had no lack of value; rather
the reverse. To the homespun man it was a success of
most excellent quality, and the chief symbol of success
in all kinds. Yearly he made his own revenues, and
his people's along with them, and as the source of them,
larger; and in all states of his revenue, he had con-
trived to make his expenditure less than it; and yearly
saved masses of coin, and ' reposited them in barrels in
the cellars of his Schloss,'—where they proved very
useful one day. Much in Friedrich Wilhelm proved
useful, beyond even his expectations. As a Nation's

Husband he seeks his fellows among kings, ancient and modern. Happy the Nation which gets such a Husband once in the half-thousand years ! The Nation, as foolish wives and nations do, repines and grudges a good deal, its weak whims and will being thwarted very often ; but it advances steadily, with consciousness or not, in the way of well doing ; and after long times the harvest of this diligent sowing becomes manifest to the nation and to all nations."

"Strange as it sounds in the Republic of Letters, we are tempted to call Friedrich Wilhelm a man of genius;—genius fated and *promoted* to work in National Husbandry, not in writing Verses or three-volume Novels. A silent genius. His melodious stanza, which he cannot bear to see halt in any syllable, is a rough fact reduced to order;—fact made to stand firm on its feet, with the world-rocks under it, and looking free towards all the winds and all the stars. He goes about suppressing platitudes, ripping-off futilities, turning deceptions inside out. The realm of Disorder, which is Unveracity, Unreality, what we call Chaos, has no fiercer enemy. Honest soul ! *and he seemed to himself such a stupid fellow often;* no tongue-learning at all ; little capable to give a reason for the faith that was in him. He cannot argue in articulate logic, only in inarticulate bellowings, or worse. He must *do* a thing, leave it undemonstrated; once done, it will itself tell what kind of thing it is, by and by. Men of genius have a hard time, I perceive, whether born on the throne or off it; and must expect contradictions next to unendurable—the plurality of blockheads being so extreme ! "

Carlyle's philosophy shines luminously clear and complete through that short extract. That is the privilege of the real doer or thinker. He gives his whole personality in each portion, however small, of his work. And, therefore, in his wisely practical manner, says Goethe— " To the higher mind even the lowest occupation is an art, for in doing one thing he does all; or to speak less paradoxically, in the one thing that he does rightly and earnestly there lies the image of all that is right." These expressions of Carlyle are, therefore, quite consonant with the preference he accords to honest, patient, hard-toiling William Burnes over the discontented, self-conscious Robert Burns; with the contempt he seems to feel for Mahomet's inspirations, and his reverence for his first fifty years of pure and blameless life; with the sneer he cannot help expressing at the high assumptions of Napoleon, and the compliment he pays him for the prudent, practical hold he held upon the real in little things, even after his frettings over insolence and insult from Sir Hudson Lowe at St. Helena. That third chapter of the fourth book of Friedrich would itself prove to any one who rightly reads it, the truth of what I have advanced regarding Carlyle's Hero-Worship.

LONDON:
PRINTED BY SMITH, ELDER AND CO.,
OLD BAILEY, E.C.

www.ingramcontent.com/pod-product-compliance
Lightning Source LLC
Chambersburg PA
CBHW030636030726
47497CB00006B/1816

www.ingramcontent.com/pod-product-compliance
Lightning Source LLC
Chambersburg PA
CBHW030636030726
47497CB00006B/1816